REINALDO ARENAS was expelled from Cuba in 1980 and now lives in New York City. His novels *Hallucinations* (1966), winner of the first prize for the best foreign novel of the year in France, and *Celestino Before Dawn* (1967) have been translated into several languages. *Farewell to the Sea* appeared in English in 1985, and his moving prose epic *El Central* was published by Avon Books in 1984.

"Through his brilliant use of the ultrarational, Arenas creates a magic world where fantasy and reality are but different views of the same existence...One of the most exciting novelists of the current Cuban crop."
Spanish American Fiction

"One of Cuba's most important unofficial writers ...Arenas bears powerful witness to the continuing, adventurous elegance of Cuban writing."
Kirkus Reviews

"Reinaldo Arenas is a young Cuban writer of tremendous talent; he is a force of nature, someone born to write."
Jose Lezama-Lima, author of *Paradiso*

"Arenas is one of the truly great writers our country has produced."
Severo Sarduay, author of
Cobra and *The Entry of Christ into Havana*

GRAVEYARD OF THE ANGELS

Reinaldo Arenas

Translated by
Alfred J. MacAdam

 AVON
PUBLISHERS OF BARD, CAMELOT, DISCUS AND FLARE BOOKS

For Dolores M. Kock,
because without her encouragement this novel would never
have been written.

GRAVEYARD OF THE ANGELS is an original publication of Avon
Books. This work has never before appeared in book form. This work is a
novel. Any similarity to actual persons or events is purely coincidental.

AVON BOOKS
A division of
The Hearst Corporation
1790 Broadway
New York, New York 10019

Copyright © 1987 by Reinaldo Arenas
English translation copyright © 1987 by Alfred J. MacAdam
Published by arrangement with the author
Library of Congress Catalog Card Number: 86-91031
ISBN: 0-380-75075-9

First Avon Printing: May 1987

AVON TRADEMARK REG. U.S. PAT. OFF. AND IN OTHER COUNTRIES, MARCA
REGISTRADA, HECHO EN U.S.A.

Printed in the U.S.A.

OPM 10 9 8 7 6 5 4 3 2 1

Angel de la jiribilla, ruega por nosotros. Y sonríe.

—José Lezama Lima

Preface

Cecilia Valdés; or, Angel Hill by the Cuban Cirilo Villaverde is one of the great novels of the nineteenth century.
Villaverde began it in Havana circa 1839, went into exile, and
finished it in New York, where it was finally published in its
entirety in 1882.

The novel has traditionally been read as a portrait of early
nineteenth-century Cuba and as an abolitionist tract, a kind of
Cuban *Uncle Tom's Cabin,* but it is much more than a period
piece or a document of social protest. *Cecilia Valdés* is the
moral mirror of a society perverted and made wealthy by slavery, and while it does describe the trials and tribulations of
slaves in Cuba during the last century, it is also a "summa of
irreverence," an attack on the conventions and mores of that
century—which, by and large, are those of our own age. To
achieve its goals, it reinterprets the idea of incest.

Incest in *Cecilia Valdés* is not limited to the half brother
and sister Leonardo and Cecilia; the entire novel is permeated
by incessant, skillfully suggested incestuous patterns. What
makes this text enigmatic and immortal is that when Villaverde presents us with a series of incestuous entanglements—
consummated or suggested—he is really showing us a unique
vision of the eternal human tragedy—man's solitude, his in-
communication, his intransferable disquiet, his quest for an
ideal lover who, because he or she is ideal, can only be a
mirror or reflection of that solitary seeker.

My re-creation of Villaverde's work is neither a condensa-
tion nor a revision of the original. I have taken his general
ideas, some of his episodes, a few of his metaphors, and let
my own imagination run wild with them. I am not offering the
reader the novel Cirilo Villaverde wrote—which is obviously
unnecessary—but the novel I would have written if I were in
his place. A betrayal, of course. But betrayal is one of the

1

preconditions of artistic creation. No work of fiction can be a transcription or reflection of a given model, not even if that model is reality itself. If it were, it would no longer be a work of fiction.

I have defined my own work here as a rewriting because that's what literature is, and the tradition goes back to the very birth of literature—or at least to the birth of great literature. It's what Aeschylus, Sophocles, and Euripides did in antiquity and what Shakespeare and Racine did later on—just to mention some of the most illustrious "rewriters" in history. To brag about original plots is a recent fallacy, one Jorge Luis Borges has brilliantly mocked. And such great Spanish-American writers as Alfonso Reyes (in *Iphigenia the Cruel*), Virgilio Piñera (in *Electra Garrigó*), and Mario Vargas Llosa (in *The War of the End of the World*) have understood that it is a fallacy. With precedents as grand as these, I don't think my own modest efforts need special justification. In any case, I believe that when we work with an already known plot as literary raw material, we can, paradoxically, be much more original because, instead of improvising something new just for the sake of novelty, we are entering into the pure essence of the imagination, that is, into genuine creation.

The "conclusions" my book reaches are exactly the ones Villaverde reached in his. I think I see in both of us a common human patrimony which we writers, modest spokesmen for that heritage, reflect: the incessant quest for liberation, a quest that in the face of ever-increasing infamies—or perhaps because of them—becomes more widespread every day.

R.A.

Part One

THE FAMILY

Chapter I

THE MOTHER

In the small room she shares with her mother, Rosario lies in bed with her newborn daughter. Suddenly she hears the noise of a carriage drawing near. Doña Josefa opens the door, and now Rosario hears the conversation between her mother and the man who was once her lover, don Cándido de Gamboa.

"I've come for the child."

"Where are you taking her?"

"First to the foundling home. I'll see she lacks for nothing, but no one must know I'm her father."

"What about Rosario?"

"She must understand that this is the only solution. She can't have imagined I would publicly recognize the child as my own. . . . Is she mad?"

Don Cándido and Josefa now enter the room. They take the baby, who cries almost unwillingly and immediately falls silent.

"Rosario," says Josefa, already at the door with her granddaughter in her arms, "this is all for the best. . . ."

Rosario doesn't speak. She closes her eyes and seems to sleep. With her eyes closed she is better able to contemplate the entire course of her life: granddaughter of a slave grandmother and an unknown white man; daughter of a dark mulatta and an unknown white man; mulatta herself, lover of a white man who is abandoning her, and mother of a baby girl who will also never know her father. Now she understands that she was only an object of pleasure for the man who is taking her child away from her, and that misery, disdain, and helplessness are her only worldly possessions. And she understands more: She understands that in the world which she inhabits there is no place for her, not even in oblivion.

She will have to go out into the city, work for, see, and

4

serve the very people who disdain and humiliate her. Hypocritically, submissively, she will have to kiss the hand she would like to see cut off, the hand she herself would like to sever.

Rosario now opens her eyes and looks toward the altar where she sees the Virgin pierced by a fiery sword holding the Child in her arms.

"What consolation," she asks herself, "can help me to go on living?"

(Because the worst of all this was not only that her child was being taken away from her, but that the child's father, the man she loved and still does love, was the person taking her baby away. And as he did it he didn't even look at her, the mother of his child.)

"Madness, madness," it seemed someone was saying to her in a low, soothing voice that lulled her and made her sleep, as she had lulled and made her lover sleep, or at least as she had lulled the fruit of their love to sleep.

"Madness, madness," someone repeated, even more soothingly, even more sweetly.

And Rosario Alarcón went mad.

Chapter II

THE FATHER

Mad, of course. Rosario had to be completely mad to think that I, don Cándido de Gamboa y Lanza, future count of Gamboa—a title I've paid a tidy sum to the king of Spain himself to get—would ever publicly recognize an illegitimate daughter. A daughter begotten on the wrong side of the sheets with a woman who is virtually black, which is what Rosario is, after all.

But things never work out for the best with these blacks: If you whip them, you're a despot; if you don't, you're a fool and they'll steal the very coals out of the kitchen stove. . . . In point of fact, I've been too good. Who in the world but me would ever think of taking care of a bastard daughter he's had with a Negress in a moment of pleasure? No one. Only Cándido Gamboa. Who has made it possible for our daughter, Cecilia, mulatta that she is, to receive a solid education at the school for orphans, and who saw to it that neither she nor her mother or grandmother ever lacked for a single thing? It's been I who've kept them all alive, with my work and my fortune. And still they speak ill of me! What did they want? Did they want me to take in Cecilia as one more of my daughters? To bring her to live in my house with my legitimate children? To let the daughter of a Negress live with my white daughters and my son, little Leonardo? Did they want my legal wife, doña Rosa de Gamboa, the future countess, to go out for a drive in her carriage with the little mulatto girl, as if she were her own daughter? What would people say? . . . Why, Cecilia might not even be my daughter. Rosario might have been made pregnant by any damn field nigger. It's the height of folly!

But in a country of blacks and mulattoes you can only expect the worst. We see a perfect example—unfortunately—in Cecilia herself, who is already twelve years old. Yes, it's

6

been twelve years since Rosario went crazy. Cecilia is almost a woman, and all she ever does is wander the streets and plazas, wear out her sandals day and night, play, both with the blacks and with the mulattoes and whites. It's easy to see she won't come to a good end.... Of course, if people find out that I'm her father, they'll say I'm a murderer because I never recognized her as my legal daughter. But the fact of the matter is that every week I visit her grandmother and give her an ounce of gold to keep her and the child. An ounce of gold! I try to keep her from keeping company with blacks or mulattoes, and I try to see she keeps regular hours. But her grandmother, good-natured Negress that she is, well, the words go in one ear and out the other.

Why, only yesterday Cecilia was here—in my own house! My daughters saw her pass by in the street and invited her in to play. They asked her a thousand questions and were charmed by the mulatta's curls. I looked at her with great misgiving, thinking all the while: *She's the very image of my daughter Adela.* . . . And I think that even my wife, who never misses a trick, noticed the resemblance and became very serious. If she finds out that the mulatta is my daughter, the family will be ruined and so will the Gamboa title. But in these parts, as they say, if you don't have Congo blood, you've got it from some other tribe. And how could it be otherwise, with those half-naked Negresses who wiggle a thousand times just walking from the kitchen to the dining room? And those bodies, those hips. . . . But I, of course, have no black blood. I'm not even a criollo, born here. I'm a pure Spaniard, and I've made my fortune with the sweat of my own brow.

I've been a bricklayer, a carpenter, I've sold lumber and roofing tiles, and, more than anything else, I've risked my fortune, and at times my very skin, importing "sacks of coal"—African blacks—and selling them to the plantation owners. I'm proud to say I've contributed to the development of this island and to the wealth of these thankless folks. It's true my marriage with Rosa helped me a great deal: She had her fortune. But I've tripled it with my work. . . . I own a plantation, a coffee plantation, a barnful of fresh blacks. I own a mansion right in the center of Havana, with a magnificent entry court and beautiful carriages. I've got my son studying in the San Carlos Seminary. And all those things I've done myself, through hard work! And they still say I'm a bad man and that I shoot my slaves through the head with the first weapon that comes to hand! Lies! I merely smash clay dishes, lanterns, copper pots, or straw chairs over their heads. Things that aren't worth much money.

Chapter III

CECILIA

She was twelve years old, and her only passion was walking; that is, wandering the tangled streets of Havana and wearing out the wooden soles of her sandals by banging them on the pavement. She would come and go from the Capitanía General to the Monserate Gate, going in and out of plazas and churches, deafening people with every step.

Sometimes, without letting her grandmother find out, she would go beyond the city wall and stroll around the Manglar district. She would even knock at the doors of private houses and then run away, leaving a cloud of dust behind, before anyone appeared. Occasionally she would slip without permission into the patio of the Belenite fathers, and would cause, as much among the young men as among the old priests themselves, an enormous fuss.

"Cecilia, Cecilia," she seemed to hear the voice of her grandmother, calling her from their house on San Juan de Dios alley. But she, Cecilia, was now speaking with don Cándido de Gamboa's daughters and, above all, with his son, Leonardo. He would take advantage of the slightest opportunity to give her a little pinch or to accompany her to the market in Plaza Vieja, where free blacks, mulattoes, and even Spaniards hawked all kinds of merchandise, from knives to peacocks, from elastic suspenders to a portable gallows.

But Cecilia's passion was not yet Leonardo but the streets. It was as if she were incapable of stopping anywhere. In the midday heat, when everyone in the city except the slaves was sleeping the siesta, the noise of her sandals resounded aggressively on the pavement, the wooden bridges, and even the clay roof tiles, which she would smash by walking on them at that hour of the day and enrage both the house owners and their slaves—who were ordered to chase after her throughout the city. They could never catch her.

9

"Cecilia," the black women call out to offer her (free) a freshly fried omelet; "Cecilia," call the girls from behind the ironwork on their windows to tease her; "Cecilia," call the boys to have her play ball with them; "Cecilia," call the old ladies to ask her how doña Josefa is getting on. . . . But she doesn't answer. Her pleasure isn't arriving at a destination but walking, running. Going on.

She knows that if she stops she'll have to answer the same old questions: "Are you black or white?" "Who is your mother?" "Who is your father?" "Who supports you?" "What's your background?" "Is it true you were in the foundling home?" And her background, at least for her, is an enigma. All she knows about her family is that she has: one mulatta grandmother, who lives on what no one knows; one black great-grandmother who some say is a witch; one scar on her right shoulder; one last name, the one she was given at her baptism in the foundling home, as is done with all children of unknown parents.

Other people have brothers, fathers, mothers, someone to hate or love, to resemble or to reject. All Cecilia has is the streets, the city gates, and the daylight. She only has herself, and that's how she knows (or intuits) that if she stops making noise she ceases to exist.

Chapter IV

THE GRANDMOTHER

When Cecilia comes home, late at night as usual, doña Josefa is still awake, waiting up for her. She fears that one day the girl will not come home. She fears—senses—that her granddaughter's fate will be like her own or like that of her daughter Rosario, or like that of her own mother: a desolate destiny.

Cecilia will fall in love with a white man who will use her as a lover; a woman to be visited in secret only when he needs to satisfy his lust.

In fact, Cecilia was already in love with a white man, although perhaps not even she knew it. But her grandmother had seen the elegant figure of a young man talking with her granddaughter through the window railings. They were whispering together, clearly not for the first time. Perhaps when she, the grandmother, was out of the house, that man had entered. Perhaps they were already lovers.

Silently, in that shadowlike way of walking so typical of her, doña Josefa reached the living room and recognized the elegant young man. It was Leonardo Gamboa—don Cándido's son, Cecilia's brother. He was the one courting her. He was the man Cecilia loved, and not exactly in a brotherly way.

No doubt about it: It was either a curse or a joke, thought the grandmother, withdrawing to her room and contemplating the Virgin pierced by a flaming sword that shone (thanks to a lighted candle) in her niche. They had hidden the identity of Cecilia Valdés's parents so well that her own brother, without knowing it, had fallen in love with her. And she with him. That was the worst part.

What would don Cándido say when he found out? Because sooner or later he would find out. . . . Perhaps he would have his daughter killed or at the least expelled from the city. He would cut off their stipend. They would die of hunger.

11

And after all—doña Josefa went on thinking—wasn't it logical that Cecilia would look for a white man? What future would she have married to a mulatto or a black in a nation where there was slavery? Maid, street vendor, seamstress, cook. Those jobs if things went well. . . . She was now eighteen years old. No one at first glance would think she had any black blood. She might even be able to marry a white, have children. So she wouldn't interfere, the grandmother would never see her again. As far as Rosario Alarcón was concerned, crazy as a loon, according to the nuns in the sanatorium for women, she could never care for her child. And Cecilia's past was only a half-moon-shaped scar that doña Josefa had cut into her shoulder so she could find Cecilia among the multitude of children of anonymous parents deposited in the foundling home.

But, of course, if, as with all the women in the family, Cecilia's fate—and desire—was to live with a white man, that man could not be her own brother, doña Josefa said to herself. Brushing aside her misgivings, she decided to visit don Cándido Gamboa immediately to see how they could put a stop to this business before something worse happened and before doña Rosa found out.

Chapter V

Doña Rosa Sandoval y de Gamboa, like all jealous women, was extremely suspicious: She never for an instant believed her husband, don Cándido Gamboa, when he would say he had a very urgent meeting with some other landowners or slave traders and leave the house for the evening. She skill-fully bribed the slave Dionysius, the master cook, a person she felt she could rely on, to disguise himself in complicated ways and spy on her husband. The results of his investigations were soon forthcoming:

"De marse done taken a beyutiful mulatta as uh mistress. She live down San Juan de Dió street an she jus' give birth to uh beyutiful little yaller gal. If you'd only uh seen huh, missy! She look jus' like miss Adela, youah own chile!"

"So don Cándido has a daughter by a nigger. . . ."

"Not uh nigguh, missy, a mulatta—"

"It's all the same, you fool!" doña Rosa interrupted him. And then, staring fixedly at the black, she ordered him, "Close the door and get undressed immediately!"

"But, missy! What ah did? All ah done was tuh folla youah orders and whut I say be de trut'. Why you gonna whip me?"

"No one's going to whip you, Dionysius," doña Rosa replied. "I've just ordered you to take your clothes off."

The black, still fearful, took off his baggy, worn-out hemp trousers, steeling himself against the lashes he thought would rain down on his back. But doña Rosa, instead of beating him, walked around him, inspecting him minutely. She felt his glands, his knees, the palms of his hands, and the soles of his feet. She made him stick out his tongue and weighed his penis and testicles several times in her hand.

As she finished this detailed review of his body, she said, "I hope you don't have any of those contagious diseases the field niggers get."

"Naw, missy, nevah, except foah duh smallpox dat I got when dey took me from Guinea."

"Good. Now listen to what you have to do: Right now you are going to possess me and make me pregnant with a black baby boy. A black boy, understand? If you don't, you'll go straight to the cane grinder out on the plantation and end up as brown sugar."

"Please, missy, not dat!"

"Shut your mouth and get to work!" doña Rosa peremptorily ordered as she took off her enormous housecoat and stood stark naked before the cringing slave.

Dionysius, still confused, hesitated, but the looks doña Rosa darted at him were so menacing that, fearing for his life, he approached his mistress's enormous body.

"Remember now, I want a black boy!" doña Rosa repeated.

"Missy, ah do' know if ah can do all dat," protested the cook.

"Shut up and get started," doña Rosa interrupted him again, "because don Cándido will be home soon, and he'll cut your head off."

Once the coupling was over, doña Rosa announced: "I hope you understand that if you breathe so much as a word about what you've done to me you'll be dead in twenty-four hours."

"Ain't done nuthin', missy," the slave protested, climbing back into his trousers.

"What do you mean *nothing*, you shameless beast?" exclaimed doña Rosa, both outraged and satisfied. "Now get out of here! Get back to the kitchen. My honor is restored."

Chapter VI

Nine months later, doña Rosa felt birth pangs and realized she simply could not give birth to a black baby in her own home. So off she went to the Church of the Angel, perched on the hill of the same name. Taking advantage of her rank, she demanded to be confessed by the bishop himself, don Manuel Morell de Ocaña y Echerre.

This singular prelate—singular as much for his ugliness as for his outrageous behavior—succeeded in moving the seat of the bishopric of Havana to Angel Hill, despite the open opposition of the marquis of Someruelos and the dowager duchess of Valero. From Angel Hill he officiated with such splendor and pomp that he even outstripped his lavish predecessor, bishop Espada.

Actually, before the advent of bishop Espada the now-famous Angel Hill in Havana did not exist. The hill in fact was a hollow. It was he who built the Church of the Angel there and he who founded the renowned cemetery that today bears his name. The dead poured into the ground beneath the church at such a rate (above all during Echerre's tenure) that the burial ground rapidly turned into a gigantic elevation on top of which the temple or nave, loaded with absolutely unnecessary columns, spires, stuccowork, gargoyles, barbicans, volutes, archivolts, rose steadily. Thus, as vault after vault filled with cadavers, the cemetery turned into one enormous tomb, and, above that conglomeration of bones, the church, which now at times touched the very clouds, continued to rise.

The name Angel Hill (and no less the eponymous church) is made of the stuff of legend. From the first years of Espada's tenure, when the elevation began to take shape, the rumor, nay, the belief began to spread that the church had been visited by an angel. Hundreds of devout ladies claimed to have

seen the beautiful angel descend from heaven above and ca-
reen into the steeple of the church—which by then had been
transformed into a cathedral by Espada's presence. Echerre,
like all churchmen, was an atheist, and labored in vain to
discover the origin and motive of the legend. All his investigations were useless. Then Echerre was summoned to administer the last rites and final confession to the dying bishop
Espada, whose place he would soon take. Echerre asked
Espada his opinion about the apparition.

"The angel exists," answered the bishop. "You see him
before you begging absolution. I am the angel."

"What do you mean, father?"

"My son," answered the moribund ecclesiastic, "I have
been observing you for many years. I know it was you who
had me exiled to Florida when the English invaded in 1762.
You are crafty, hypocritical, ambitious, a traitor, impious, an
exhibitionist, ugly, an intriguer, and cruel. You have other
virtues, but these immediately caught my eye. And that is
why it is no accident that the bishopric of Havana, one of the
richest in the New World, will fall to you.

"For that very reason, I have summoned you to hear my
last confession, whose theme is precisely the one that has
obsessed you: the belief (the fanatical, passionate belief)
these frivolous folks hold about the visitation by the beautiful
angel. . . . When I was very young, I understood after reading
the Church Fathers that where apparitions are concerned the
ones people accept most easily are the most unbelievable and,
above all, the most agreeable. That's why I started the rumor
that this place was holy and protected by a guardian angel
during my campaign to have the cemetery that today bears my
name built here and to stop burials in Havana Cathedral,
where there wasn't room for one more body, where the stench
infected the whole city, and, above all, where no one paid fees
or tithes for souls of the dear departed. But even the old ladies
laughed at me.

"That's when I decided to give them incontrovertible evi-
dence. I dressed up as an angel and nightly wandered the
towers and balconies of the nave. The ladies went into rap-
tures at my presence. They began to bring mummies and skel-
etons over here. The angel got so famous he couldn't limit
himself to the holy nave. Wearing my splendid robes, I would
venture out into the city almost every night and appear on the

balconies of the most devout, most beautiful, and richest ladies. I don't suppose I have to tell you about the obedience and devotion with which a beautiful woman attends an angel who enters her boudoir at midnight. Yes, brother, I have angelically possessed practically every woman in this city and —oh, I wouldn't dare confess it if I weren't going to expire at any moment—many, many illustrious and highly respectable men who also didn't want to be deprived of that consolation. . . .

"Naturally, many ladies came to me seeking help so that I could get them out of the difficulty the angel had caused in their wombs. I consoled them all. I solved the problems of the married women by absolving them and then baptizing one more supposedly legitimate child. The unmarried women had to enter the convent which I had built out back for just that purpose. Thanks to those ladies, the church is now filled with nuns, altar boys, sacristans, gravediggers, coachmen, and gardeners—all of whom are supplied by those ladies and supported by their charitable gifts. I am not exaggerating, my dear brother, when I tell you that most of the citizens of this city, despite their skepticism and antireligious sentiments, have an angel for a father. Now you can see that my apostolic labors have been praiseworthy: Not only have I propagated the faith but I have populated the city with little angels as well."

Here bishop Espada, moribund as he was, could not keep from smiling. Then he went on. "Now, brother, I am leaving you. But it is my wish that the legend I have created not disappear with my body. Here is the key to the chest, that one over there in the second row on the right. Inside you will find my angelic robes. Put them on right now, because I must see if they fit you or if they will have to be altered. You are my replacement."

Genuinely excited and beaming, Echerre didn't waste a second. He opened the chest and put on the angel costume. He even added a scepter and a halo. Splendidly attired, he returned to the dying bishop. *"Bellum! Bellissimus!"* the prelate exclaimed in his professional jargon. "Now, dressed as you are, climb the steeple and announce the news of my death to the city. But absolve me first."

That afternoon the people of Havana were truly dazzled when they saw the bells of the Church of the Angel being rung by the angel himself, who had come to announce the death of the celebrated bishop Espada and, perhaps, his future canonization.

And now it was the new bishop—and new angel as well —who was inside the confessional listening, first distractedly, then with some interest, to doña Rosa de Gamboa's confession.

"Father, I have sinned."

"Daughter, it is for sinners to repent, for the repentant to receive absolution, and for those absolved to reach the kingdom of heaven.... What have you done? When? And how often?"

"Only once, father. But it wasn't for pleasure; not even because I was tempted. It was for revenge. I mean, for justice' sake."

"My daughter, being moral means not letting others see that we are as immoral as they are, and in this your social rank can help you to a great extent.... But tell me now, what is the nature of your sin?"

"It is of my own nature—I mean that it's in my womb right now and just about to come out into the world."

"And who is the author? That is, if you have any idea."

"Heavens, father! Of course I know who it is! It is my black cook."

"The black Dionysius! The best cook in Havana. I hope you don't plan to kill him!" Bishop Echerre shouted this last sentence because he was, among other things, a gourmet.

"It's true he is the best cook we've ever had, father."

"And he works outside the kitchen as well to bring his domestic labors to the peak of perfection. Your husband don Cándido does not deserve this treatment."

"But he is the real guilty party! He took his pleasure with a black woman! All I did was satisfy the needs of my pride!"

"Well, I hope your pride has had a pleasant sufficiency," said the bishop, pointing his index finger at doña Rosa's prominent belly. "That's enough. Let's go to the convent. The nuns will take good care of you. They are experts in this sort of thing because not a day passes but they have to help some lady in the same situation!"

Doña Rosa and the tall, thin bishop walked through the nave of the church, went out into the patio planted with gigantic gladioli (the prelate's favorite flower), and traversed most of the Espada Cemetery. They saw hundreds of blacks and mulattoes working to pile up huge quantities of skulls in the corners of the burial ground, while in the center they could see four enormous pyramids of bones.

"Study them well," said the bishop, peevishly pointing to the workers carrying bones from one place to another. "Even though people might not want to believe it, here in the church and cemetery you can see almost all the children of Havana's aristocracy ["and of the bishop," he added under his breath] hard at work."

"My God, father . . . !"

"Yes, daughter. If all the coachmen, cooks, peddlers, and other slaves were white, the nobles of Havana would have many more children than those they recognize. And I would have fewer employees. . . . As for *your black,*" the bishop said, emphasizing the key words, as he stopped in the very center of the elevated cemetery to contemplate the city below, which seemed to be running so quickly beneath a mantle of pure white clouds, "you ought to rein him in and make him understand in no uncertain terms that *he* is at your mercy and not the other way around. And no more visits! What with the children the angel and the slaves beget on the ladies around here, there's no more room for the dead!"

Before disappearing with doña Rosa into the convent, the bishop once again pointed toward the immense stacks of bones the workers incessantly enlarged.

That very afternoon, doña Rosa gave birth in the convent of Angel Hill to a charming mulatto the bishop himself baptized with the name José Dolores. To avoid having any suspicion fall on the Gamboas—doña Rosa had stayed in the convent for two days—he gave the baby to Merced Pimienta, a very devout black woman whose husband, the black Malanga Pimienta, had run away when he learned that his wife, too, had been "visited" by the angel. She had presented him with an almost-white little mulatto girl, Nemesia Pimienta, who was certainly not the child of an African father.

Merced Pimienta would die of sadness because the angel —who found her enjoying herself with Uribe the tailor— never visited her again. She never knew the true identity of the parents of the cute mulatto boy, José Dolores Pimienta, whom she raised with great difficulty along with the child Nemesia he thought of and loved as a sister. Although from time to time master Uribe (who thought he was Nemesia's father) and bishop Echerre (who knew he was her father) contributed to the support of the orphans until José Dolores could make a living on his own.

As for doña Rosa de Gamboa: After she handed the sum required in such cases over to bishop Echerre, she went down on her knees to receive absolution. Relieved (and lighter), she returned home, where no one—except the cook Dionysius—noticed any change in her. Doña Rosa was so fat that the eight or nine pounds she had lost in two days made no difference in her figure.

It is only proper we note that she was never again unfaithful to her husband.

Chapter VII

A FAMILY GATHERING

Lunch, which had begun at eleven o'clock in the morning, went on until after the stroke of one. Everyone was sitting at table, waiting for the candied egg yolks, a special dessert only one cook in Havana knew how to prepare—the slave Dionysius.

At the head of the table was don Cándido; to his right, doña Rosa and their son, Leonardo. To don Cándido's left were seated the three daughters of the family, Antonia, Carmen, and Adela. At the far end of the table was the Spanish majordomo, don Manuel Reventós. Behind the family, carrying things to and fro, indefatigable and silent, were the domestic slaves, led by Dionysius himself and by Tirso, a young slave who waited on don Cándido exclusively.

Tirso was so skillful in serving that don Cándido had only to make the slightest gesture and Tirso knew whether he wanted the three-legged brazier to light a cigar, the gigantic silver brush with golden bristles so his back could be scratched, or the modern flyswatter so he could smash those officious bugs that buzzed so energetically around the prominent nostrils of the young ladies. In truth, the lad was always at the ready, attentive almost twenty-four hours a day to his master's winks and nods.

The conversation, as usual in the Gamboa household at lunch and dinner, ran to domestic themes, so the majordomo, while he had the honor to sit at their table, did not take part in it, unless, of course, don Cándido or doña Rosa addressed him directly.

"Mommy," said Leonardo as he finished his fifth candied egg yolk swimming in Spanish oil and local brandy, "some new Swiss repeater watches, the best in the world, have just arrived at Dubois's jewelry store."

"Don't think we're going to buy you another watch!"

screeched don Cándido. As he shouted he made a gesture that young Tirso interpreted as a request for the hot coals, which the servant promptly stuck right under his nose. "Ah, you dog!" bellowed don Cándido, snatching the gigantic brazier and throwing it at the slave's head. Tirso survived only because he had been dodging blows like that all his life. Then don Cándido, even angrier because he'd burned his fingers when he grabbed the brazier, began to pound the table, knocking some plates to the floor. "No watch, no watch!" And, addressing Leonardo: "What do you think this is? Do you think we own all the silver mines in Peru?"

"What a way to talk to our little Leonardo!" interjected doña Rosa. "You'd think Leonardo weren't your own son."

"You're to blame because you've spoiled him: Instead of thinking about your daughters, you only think about him!" declared don Cándido, standing up and hugging his eldest daughter, Antonia.

"And you never think about Leonardo!" said doña Rosa with a loving look at her son.

"My girls deserve a better mother than the one they have." Don Cándido sighed tragically, embracing each one of his daughters so tightly that he almost suffocated them to death.

Then doña Rosa, who would never be second to her husband in anything, stood up and, dripping perspiration, spun her son around, hugging him again and again against her enormous bosom.

"Chocolate!" shouted don Cándido Gamboa. And at the mention of that word, peace was restored.

Two black maids in long dresses painfully dragged in an immense caldron where the chocolate and milk bubbled. Still boiling, the liquid was transferred to large porcelain cups and from there it was poured down the respective throats of the family members. The family drank it at such a high temperature because of a tradition don Cándido had inherited in his native land.

At the end of dinner, the heat of the outside world combined with that of their almost incandescent bodies, with the result that the thick bodies were almost swimming in their own perspiration.

"Don Reventós!" doña Rosa thundered, as if the majordomo were a mile off.

"Ma'am?"

"Take these twenty ounces of gold, go straight to Dubois's, and buy me the best repeater watch. Tell Dubois it's for me so they won't try to cheat you."

"Don Reventós!" thundered don Cándido even more loudly. "If you obey this madwoman's order I'll see you get five hundred lashes."

"Sir!"

"Reventós!" shouted doña Rosa in a frenzy. "I want that repeater watch right away, or you're going out to the plantation to work on the cane grinder."

"Ma'am!"

"I'm going up to take a siesta," said Leonardo Gamboa in a bored voice, knowing that the argument could go on all afternoon. He kissed doña Rosa and went up to his room.

"Reventós, Reventós!" shouted don Cándido in a still-louder voice so his son would be unable to sleep. "I'm the master in this house, and if you buy the watch, I'm going to put you on all fours and whip you as if you were a black fresh from Africa!"

"Reventós," said doña Rosa in a low voice, so she would not interrupt her son's nap, "you should already be on your way back here, or is it that you want to go to the grinder? Just wait until you've had a taste of that. Do you know what turning into 'brown sugar' means?"

The majordomo knew the answer to that question and turned completely pale. Without waiting another instant, he began to run to the jeweler. "Take one more step and I'll kill you!" don Cándido immediately shouted, pulling out an enormous salt pistol (which he always wore in his belt to strike fear into the slaves). He filled its chambers with salt from the huge saltcellar on the table and took aim at the majordomo's head.

Then don Reventós, knowing he was in a life-or-death situation, or rather a death-or-death situation, said:

"I see that for you, sir and madam, the central issue here, the one my life hinges on, is whether or not I go to Mr. Dubois's jewelry shop *to buy a watch*. Isn't that the case?"

"Exactly," said don Cándido. "If you go, I'll kill you."

"As for me," replied doña Rosa, "you know what's waiting for you. . . ."

"Then the problem is solved," said the majordomo in a

triumphant voice. Without further ado, he summoned the cook Dionysius.

"Yessir?" said the black, dripping with sweat.

"Take these twenty ounces of gold. That's twenty ounces, now! Take them to the jewelry shop on Muralla street and bring madam here the best repeater watch in the place. Now get moving, understood?"

"Yes, sir," said the slave, leaving at top speed.

"Do you see, sir and madam, how the problem is solved and how I've saved my life?" the majordomo explained in professorial style. "I've neither gone to the jeweler's—as evidenced by the fact that I'm still here—nor have I not gone, since at any time now the new repeater watch will be here."

When he heard the majordomo's ingenious rationalization, don Cándido thought he would explode and raised his hands to his head. That gesture was Tirso's cue to scratch the master's back, which he immediately began to do, using the immense brush.

That mistake by the slave was don Cándido's cue to grab the brush furiously and throw it so violently into the entry court that it knocked over and killed one of the Spanish mares, affectionately nicknamed Carmen Balcels, which was tied up next to the buggy in anticipation of the young ladies' afternoon ride.

The fatally wounded animal gave a stentorian whinny and expired, causing the three young ladies to weep uncontrollably, especially Carmen, don Cándido's favorite, who (perhaps because she had the same name) was especially fond of the poor beast.

Her father, deeply moved by his daughters' weeping and the sight of them clinging to the animal's cadaver, regained his composure, called for silence, asked for his dearest daughter's forgiveness, and went upstairs, ready to sleep away the siesta.

Part Two

THE BLACKS AND
THE WHITES

Chapter VIII

THE BALL

Cecilia's passion is no longer wearing out her sandals on the streets but dancing. Eighteen years old, skin the color of bronze, tall, slender, with black hair, she is the center of attraction at every dance. The blacks woo her respectfully, as something impossible; the mulattoes, knowing they are her equals, treat her with a certain complicity and familiarity that make Cecilia indignant. As for the whites, they think they are honoring the mulatta by condescending to come to black dances just to dance with her.

This evening's party takes place in the house of Mercedes Ayala, "a mulatta so high yellow she's gold," as her intimate friend Cantalapiedra, the police chief in the Angel neighborhood, described her. The invited guests began to arrive in the afternoon. Mulattas wrapped in multicolored shawls they coquettishly let slip, revealing their bare shoulders as they wave beautiful fans; mulattoes wearing high, shiny boots, top hats, and extremely tight jackets that outline their athletic bodies; blacks scrupulously turned out in white: They fill all the rooms illuminated by large crystal chandeliers ablaze with tallow candles.

While it's rare—almost impossible—to see white women at these balls for "colored people," there are many young white men, many from the best families in Havana, who pursue, usually with success, one or more of these beautiful mulattas.

Among those young men is the elegant Leonardo Gamboa, impeccably dressed in Parisian style, with kidgloves, and a gold-handled, mother-of-pearl walking stick. He is surrounded by a retinue of friends as elegant and insolent as himself. The clothes worn by almost all these bravos is made by Uribe, a free black who, helped by José Dolores Pimienta, has had great success and runs his own tailoring establishment. He too is at the party.

At around ten o'clock, Cecilia Valdés, accompanied by her friend Nemesia Pimienta, alights from a two-wheeled carriage.

The entrance of Cecilia, a young lady who looks absolutely white, in a dance where there are only black and mulatto women, causes a sensation. She is wearing a gown of polka-dotted tulle with short sleeves and puffed shoulders, with a long white skirt, a black velvet hat decorated with feathers and real flowers, felt slippers, white, elbow-length gloves, and a long, wide red belt that cinches her waist.

Mercedes Ayala herself interrupts her animated conversation with Cantalapiedra and steps to the center of the hall to embrace Cecilia.

Then the musicians, led by José Dolores Pimienta, burst into song with an enormous blast of violins, drums, clavichords, clarinets, and cellos.... It's true they've been playing for hours, but it is equally true that with the appearance of Cecilia Valdés the spirit of the music (and the musicians) acquires such liveliness that it seems that only now has the orchestra begun to play with genuine mastery.

Numerous mulattoes and blacks, all ceremonious and impeccable, greet Cecilia. Among them the elegant and excellent musician Brindis de Sala and the young and lissome captain Tondá (a protégé of the captain general himself), who has just completed his nightly tour of the entire city. Also coming to greet Cecilia are the black poets Gabriel de la Concepción Valdés (who was nursed with Cecilia in the foundling home) and Francisco Manzano, now free and earning his living as a pastry cook—his confections may be tasted at the long table in the hall, which is piled high with all sorts of food and drink.

The orchestra stops playing for a moment, and José Dolores Pimienta also runs to greet his beloved Cecilia, whom he calls "my little bronze virgin." Cecilia doesn't find the nickname flattering since it reminds her of her black blood. And it is now when the handsome adolescent that Leonardo Gamboa still is takes Cecilia's hand and kisses it devoutly right in front of the astonished José Dolores.

As if that weren't enough, Cecilia turns toward the mulatto and admonishes him:

"Well now. Is this how a man should keep his word?"

"I've always kept my word," responds José Dolores, disconcerted.

"Is that so?" says Cecilia as she fans herself with one hand and holds Leonardo's with the other. "And the contradanse you promised to play?"

When the others hear Cecilia request a contradanse, they all, bored with the ceremonious minuet, begin to shout, "Yes, yes, the contradanse, the contradanse, we want something modern!" The result is that José Dolores Pimienta not only has to leave Cecilia in the arms of his rival, but he also has to play a pretty contradanse for them to dance to.

Chapter IX

JOSÉ DOLORES

Ever since he was a boy, José Dolores had loved Cecilia Valdés. Knowing how ambitious she was, he had learned various skills, from tailoring to church organist at the Angel Hill church, from orchestra leader to hat maker and sandal vendor. By means of all those jobs he supported Nemesia Pimienta and saved a few ounces of gold for the wedding—should Cecilia ever decide to marry him.

And tonight, just when, according to Nemesia, Cecilia was about to give in, out of nowhere comes this rich white playboy. And he, the mulatto, not only has to remain silent but also must provide a musical accompaniment to his disgrace.

And what music! Stupendous, fast contradanses that set all the dancers into motion. Then he moved on to some Cuban dances, livelier still. Soon there was nothing but a whirlwind of incessantly moving feet.

They danced in the brightly lit hall, in the darker rooms, in the dark corridors, in the patio, the garden, and, now, in the dark street itself. The rain turned the entire house into an almost impassable swamp which the elegant ladies with their trains and the gentlemen with their already muddy boots constantly stirred up.

Never ceasing to play his clarinet, Pimienta could see Cecilia and Leonardo in a tight embrace amidst that furor of tangling and untangling couples. In one of those violent whirls, carried away by the rhythm or pushed by the other dancers, the couple whizzed by, under the very nose of the musician. Above the orchestra's noise, Pimienta heard Leonardo say words that were a slap in the face for him: "Don't forget to leave the door ajar so that when the old lady goes out I can come in. . . ." "I won't forget," said Cecilia, clasping Leonardo's jacket, a jacket, just to top things off perfectly,

29

which was the very one that he, José Dolores Pimienta, had sewn at the order of master Uribe.

It was then that the mulatto, possessed by an insatiable grief, began to play the clarinet with enormous power and virtuosity, drawing from it such harmonies that all those who passed by the house got out of their carriages or buggies (if they happened to be riding) and began to dance.

By then it was impossible to tell the invited guests from the crashers. The music that emerged from José Dolores Pimienta's instrument had taken control of everyone. People were dancing on top of the chairs, on top of the well, on the stairs, on the roof, and even up in the trees. Just to give some idea of the multitude crammed in there.

The most unusual aspect of this real event was not only the furor caused by those melodies, but that their magic seemed endless. The people had been dancing frenetically for five hours and no one gave any sign of fatigue. It's true that a few centenarian Negresses had dropped dead beneath the confused feet of the dancers, but even as they expired they gave one last shake, a sign that meant they were dying completely happy. Their bodies were removed with a thunderous round of applause and without any interruption of the dancing.

Inspired by Pimienta, the musicians, still playing their many kinds of instruments (wind, bronze, skin, wood, stone), slipped among the dancers and moved so frenetically that at times, because of those vertiginous whirls, they soared up to the beams of the high-ceilinged mansion, some of them getting caught on the ridgepole where, upside down, they kept on playing and frenetically shaking, like bats possessed by the god of dance.

Only José Dolores Pimienta, impressive in his leather boots, black swallowtail coat, and linen trousers, kept his place on the bandstand, pouring out that noisy but—in the last analysis—sentimental music.

Chapter X

NEMESIA PIMIENTA

Her function, it seemed, was not to live but merely to exist, occasionally to serve. She wasn't born to shine but to remain in the shadows, like those opaque and cloudy shapes that dissolve anonymously behind the major figures in great paintings, whose function it is to be mere silhouettes, distance markers, aids to make what is really important stand out from the background.

Who cared (except her) about her frustrated love, her unfulfilled desires, her whims and anxieties that no one ever tried to satisfy? Cecilia would dance, and all around her it was either applause or envy. Cecilia would laugh, and everyone would try to find out why so they could laugh along with her. Cecilia would become angry or sad, and everyone's face would become gray and upset because of the beautiful mulatta's disquiet. But as for her, Nemesia Pimienta, whose figure and face were insignificant, whose hair was curlier and whose skin was darker, who would ever take notice of her sadness or her (highly unlikely) joy?

When they stepped down from the carriage (she behind Cecilia like a shadow), for which one were all the helping hands if not for the svelte mulatta? To whom were all the flirtatious remarks addressed if not to the more beautiful of the two women?

It seems doubtful that she, Nemesia Pimienta, was beautiful, even if the very author of the novel took great pains to suggest it—perhaps out of pity or perhaps because of literary convention. It just wasn't the case. Short ("the little old lady" is what the other Negresses in the tenement called her), insignificant, she didn't even have Cecilia's pretty voice, much less her way of walking, of laughing, not even remotely those seductive eyes.

And nevertheless, within the minuscule body there was a

31

huge heart and a no less disproportionate desire and sensuality (precisely because it had never been satisfied) than that in—as she herself thought—Cecilia. Her need for love was naturally more unbridled and hysterical than that of other women, especially those who either already had or could have anything—or almost anything—they wished. Nemesia's ambitions might have been less outrageous than Cecilia's, but they were no more feasible for being more modest.

Nemesia Pimienta did not aspire, as did Cecilia, to be Leonardo Gamboa's wife; she didn't even aspire to be his official mistress. She only hoped to be his temporary lover, so that for a single moment she could unleash all his passion. . . . How her eyes pursued that exemplar of masculine beauty! Every step he took, every gesture he made, stirred her desperation and her desire. . . . Go-between, messenger, pander running back and forth between Cecilia and Leonardo: That's what she became. She submitted herself to every humiliation and would go on submitting herself as long as she could see young Gamboa. Perhaps, she thought, she might even get to touch his hand. But he, impassive, never noticed her, never acted as if he knew she was there.

Then, momentarily convinced that Leonardo Gamboa would never possess her, she dreamed of other loves that were a sublimation of her great love. And, regardless of risk, she tried to make her dreams realities. At midnight, she would walk along the city walls and then go beyond them to the Manglar district and even to the slave barracks. A man, a young man, white, mulatto, even a black, as long as he was handsome. A warm and loving body, a body that, when it clasped her, would quench (if only for an instant) her body's passion. A body that for a moment would caress her, protect her, would sink into her body, dominate it, and infuse it with plenitude and calm. . . . But nothing like that ever happened, and Nemesia Pimienta, small, dark, and filled with desire, would return home, where her supposed brother, José Dolores, was already asleep.

Watching him breathe, she slowly approached his bed. *If her brother, her handsome brother, so different from her, loved her not as a sister* . . . José Dolores, José Dolores, now he was the man of her dreams. And once again Nemesia Pimienta kissed the young man, who went on sleeping. "Cecilia, Cecilia," José Dolores would sometimes say in his sleep as he would unknowingly embrace Nemesia. "Yes . . ." Nemesia would answer in a low voice as she went to his bed.

A man, any man. Swarthy, black, Chinese, white, an Arab. A man she could serve and adore, for whom she could wait and to whom she could give herself. A lover, a traveler, a stranger, a runaway slave, an escaped prisoner who in the rainy night would ask her for shelter. A murderer, a criminal. . . . And once again Nemesia would devotedly sew up José Dolores's trousers. She would flirt with master Uribe right in the tailor shop (he, he was the man she loved now). Sexily dressed, she strolled all around Mercedes Ayala's ballroom, her eyes seeking, demanding a corresponding pair of eyes, but the more she strove to stand out, the greater was the indifference with which she was received. She had submitted completely to that all-too-human situation of being denied what she begged and desiring those who disdained her. . . . A body, a solitary accomplice of a body with which to free herself from solitude, that was love for her, nothing else, but—for that very reason—she could never find it.

Dressed even more provocatively, she would slip out of the tenement or ball at midnight to catch and besiege the mulatto Polanco (he, the mulatto, was now the man of her dreams) on the Callejón de San Juan de Dios. She would open wide her robe and offer herself naked to the black Tondá (he, he was now the man she idolized). She ran under the full moon, which got more and more immense and threatening, and went down on her knees before commissioner Cantalapiedra as he walked down the stairs of Angel Hill, begging him, ordering him, to take her right there on the cobblestones. He, that man and no other, was now the one she loved. . . . But all of them had some excuse, some pretext, some urgent business to take care of, a dying relative, a jealous wife who was always chasing after them, a criminal who had to be executed, or some unpostponable matter to dispatch. And it was she who was always postponed, burning and cast aside, without resolution or redemption. And so her passion, her desire, her love, her need to seek and to find, became even more pressing. . . . Ah, if someone only understood that of all lovers she was the purest because she lived not for one lover but for absolute love, the supreme symbol, that like a god could become flesh and show himself through any body.

On the other hand, she had such a limited space in which

to bring her desires to fruition. No one was interested in her as a person. If anyone invited her it was because they thought of her as a kind of lady-in-waiting to Cecilia Valdés. Even the women looked on her more as a domestic utensil than as a woman. And as far as her discourse (her complaint) is concerned, well, we'll have to cut it short, in view of the fact that not even the author of the novel in which she is an insignificant element was interested in her tragedy.

He was indifferent to Nemesia Pimienta and only used her (as he did with all the rest). A love like hers, as vast and desperate as her own life, doesn't even enter—not in the slightest—in the pretentious series of chapters the author entitled "On Love." And yet her love, Nemesia protested, was greater than that of all the other characters put together. Much greater! . . . But now she saw how the pitiless author of the novel came toward her threateningly. No, she couldn't add another word; she would not be able to go on telling her tragedy, her love, her hatred to another soul. There wouldn't even be a shriek at the end of a chapter. Nothing. In an instant her mouth would be sealed and the others wouldn't even realize she had been gagged and liquidated in such a vile fashion. And all her passion, all her furor, all her tenderness would be reduced to . . .

Chapter XI

DIONYSIUS

When the slave Dionysius returned with the repeater watch, he noted with pleasure that the masters were asleep. He gave the watch and the change to don Reventós, who shot him a sarcastic, funerary glance. As he ran to the kitchen he realized his time left on earth was limited, that as soon as don Cándido woke up and found out that he had satisfied doña Rosa's caprice, he would be killed. Perhaps, so as not to infuriate doña Rosa, don Cándido would not assassinate Dionysius outright: His demise would seem unexpected, "unforeseen," like the death of the slave poet Lezama.

He knew how the masters managed things. He hadn't been a cook for more than twenty years in that family for nothing. . . . He knew that a slave in disgrace is a dead man, and that if a dispute arises involving master, lady, and slave, it's the slave who always gets the blame. He also put into practice that proverb he had learned from the whites: "Assume the worst and you'll probably be right."

So Dionysius got ready to run away. While everyone slept (even the majordomo was nodding in the dining room), he would slip out of the city, hide out in the hills, and become a *cimarrón*, a runaway slave. For the first time in his life, he would be a free man.

What was he leaving behind? Stocks, whippings, insults, and incessant labor. Even his wife, the black María Regla, had been sent, as punishment, out to the plantation when doña Rosa found her breast-feeding Cecilia, then just a few days old. And even though she was feeding Cecilia at the express order of Cándido Gamboa, no one could keep María Regla from being sent for life to La Tinaja, where slaves were worked to death in the mill eighteen hours a day.

He still remembered (with each passing day the memory became clearer) that scene. María Regla was baby Adela's wet nurse, since her mother, doña Rosa, refused to breast-feed her because "I don't want *my* breasts to sag." One night, when the mistress thought she heard a strange crying, she walked into the slave's room and found her feeding two baby girls, one on each side. One was Cecilia Valdés, the other Adela Gamboa. The row doña Rosa raised was so huge that the captain general himself sent his personal guards to find out what was going on. . . . From that moment, Dionysius never saw his wife again. What is worse, he knew she was unfaithful to him, and not with just one man. Nor was it with blacks, but with any white man who crossed her path. . . . Run away: That was the solution. He was leaving nothing behind, not even the memory of a faithful wife.

He quickly took off his slave clothes and put on a green suit that belonged to Leonardo Gamboa and which was a bit tight for him. Then he pulled on an enormous pair of boots, and added don Cándido's gold spurs for good measure. He studied his reflection in the bottom of a copper pot and tried to smooth out his kinky hair with don Cándido's gigantic gold and silver brush. But the kinks would just not go away, but he kept the brush in any case, stuffing it into the big red sack he used for marketing. As he went through the deserted rooms he continued throwing things into his sack: Leonardo's old watch, a few silver coins, some tallow candles, six bottles of wine, a live hen that was flapping about in the outer court, the long knife he used in the kitchen, and even a suckling pig don Cándido was fattening for New Year's Day, when they would return from their Christmas holiday out in the country. . . . Finally, Dionysius casually snatched up a high hat someone had left on a chair and walked out to the street.

To escape he'd have to find those places where the city wall was poorly guarded, so he headed for the poor neighborhoods, where only blacks and mulattoes lived. It was there, after walking for hours and after crossing a street where the mud reached his knees, that he was surprised and charmed by a rhythm he had never before heard. It was a music that awoke in him unknown secret anxieties that paralyzed him and then forced him to listen and obey it. . . . Unable to contain himself, Dionysius, with his sack on his back, pushed through the crowd that had gathered there and entered into the hall where José Dolores Pimienta—his unknown son—was still playing the clarinet.

Chapter XII

THE DUEL

The dancing at Mercedes Ayala's house was so frenetic and wild that the presence of that long black stuffed into a tight green swallowtail coat, wearing hip-length riding boots, gold spurs, a high hat, and carrying an enormous red sack in which an infuriated hog was grunting and a hen was clucking attracted no attention at all.

No sooner did Dionysius see Cecilia Valdés dancing with Leonardo than a hatred held in check over many years erupted. Forgetting he was a runaway, he approached the couple.

"Kin ah hav duh pleasure uv dis dance?" he asked Cecilia as he tapped her on the shoulder.

Leonardo and Cecilia were astonished by the strange figure. Cecilia reacted first:

"I'm so sorry. But can't you see that I'm already dancing with this gentleman?"

"Dat uh lie!" shouted Dionysius. "You don' wanna dance wit' me 'cause ah'm black, but let me tell you dat you black too!"

"What have I done for you to offend me in this way?" replied Cecilia indignantly.

"Mouah dan you tink. 'Cause uh you, ah had tuh be unfait'ful to ma wife, and ah been sep'rate from huh foah eighteen yeahs."

On hearing this, Leonardo fixed his startled eyes on Cecilia.

"I don't even know him. This man is mad," said Cecilia to Leonardo.

"It youah momma dat crazy! An' it youah fault!" shouted the black.

"It's you who's mad," Cecilia shouted back, so loudly that José Dolores Pimienta stopped playing his clarinet. Which meant that the entire orchestra fell silent and the dancers stopped dead in their tracks.

"Come, come, show some respect for the lady," said Leonardo Gamboa, who, out of confusion and fear, did not recognize the cook.

At that moment, the hog, which was very uncomfortable traveling inside the sack, gave such a grunt that Gamboa, scared out of his wits and thinking that the black was Lucifer himself, jumped back (knocking several people over in the process) and ran for his life. Already at some distance, he shouted to Cecilia Valdés, "Remember, I'll see you tomorrow, early in the morning!"

"See?" Dionysius said then. "You got tuh choose 'tween a coward and uh poor guy like me."

"That's where you're mistaken!" shouted Cecilia. "He is no coward!"

"Ah ain't wrong. Dey's all cowards aroun' heah. Y'all got uh yalla streak uh mile wide down youah backs!"

As he said this Dionysius shot a challenging look around the room.

"You're the coward, picking on a lady." José Dolores Pimienta leapt forward, eager to show Cecilia that he was braver than Leonardo.

"Yalla!" was Dionysius's answer. "Come on outside an' lemme let some air outta yuh."

José Dolores really would have had to be a coward not to have answered Dionysius's challenge. Father and son walked out to the street, followed by the euphoric crowd that stood off at a prudent distance.

"Mistuh Jacket, why don't you let that man out!" shouted José Dolores, ridiculing Dionysius's outfit.

"Now we see who get let out," answered Dionysius. As he opened the sack to get out his knife, the flapping chicken fluttered out and hit Cecilia Valdés square on the chest. She screamed and fainted dead away.

Cecilia had to look after herself, because the two men were already tangled up in a duel to the death. They both held their hats in their left hand as shields, and jumped toward or away from each other as they slashed and missed.

"Hurray!" shouted the crowd, which had taken cover behind the carriages and even on the roof, each time one of the fighters (it didn't matter which) sliced at the other. In any

ase, the absolute lack of streetlights made it impossible to see
vho was wounding whom. What was clear was that Diony-
ius lacked the mulatto's skill and his youth, and the immense
ack, which he preferred not to put down, made him much
ess agile. Soon everyone heard the noise of fabric ripping,
ollowed by a howl.

"Hurrah!" the crowd shouted again, without knowing
vhich had fallen.

It was Dionysius, and he landed flat on his back, finally
etting go of the red sack, out of which the hog escaped at top
peed.

"Are you hurt?" shouted Cecilia Valdés to the hog, which
t that moment ran right between her legs and which she mis-
ook for José Dolores.

"Not a scratch," answered the mulatto, emerging from
mong the shadows. "Not a nick," he added, even prouder of
imself as he felt the head of the woman he loved so deeply
esting on his breast.

They stood like that for only an instant, because another
hout came from the crowd:

"Run for it, here comes Tondá!"

And everyone, including the mortally wounded slave, scat-
ered when the elegant black captain, on horseback and com-
lete with saber and epaulets, burst onto the scene.

Chapter XIII

ON LOVE

José Dolores Pimienta would play the clarinet and she, Cecilia, would sing and dance for him. José Dolores Pimienta would arrive home at nightfall, tired from having sewn so many suits for other people, but she, Cecilia, dressed in white, with a flower in her hair, would be waiting for him at the door.... Where would the house be? On the Belén hills? Among the trees beyond the city walls? Near one of the lakes in the Manglar district? Or near the beach, where they'd go to sit at night? ... A love, a great love, had to be for him, for José Dolores Pimienta, a consolation, a shared quietude, a kind of small, modest, and magic place, safe from the horror and humiliation that surrounded him. Because a great love, he would say to himself, had to be based on a balance between two similar sensibilities marked by the same astonishment, proscribed by the same world, marked by an unjust curse, accomplices, and therefore enemies of the same history.

A party, a walk along the beach, a gathering of friends. And they always apparently near the others, but inaccessible and invulnerable, imbued (even in a crowd) with each other within that unique place accessible only to lovers.... A love, a great love, what was it but the enjoyable, tranquil, and repeated pleasure of each minute shared with the one we love? The fortune of sitting together at table, the luck of being alive and embracing, the pleasure of not living except one in the other. Because a love, precisely because it is great, can only stir small ambitions and easily satisfied pleasures. What did the world and its ambitions and madness matter, who cared for palaces, jewels, and travel, if they could enjoy the unusual treasure of an exclusive and shared affection? Nothing could equal the richness and plenitude of giving free rein

40

to one's passions, of recognizing and completing each other mutually.

Children would come, grandchildren; they would grow old. They would remember (and recount) how they met, when they fell in love. They would always be that way, leaning on each other even with their eyes. Because a love, a great love, had to be not only adventure but shared constancy and dedication, tranquillity, satisfaction, hope, and sacrifice.

Confronted by the vast panorama of solitude and despair, of ambition and crime, they, with their passion, would erect a wall and live (and die) in its shadow, together.

Those were José Dolores Pimienta's thoughts, and his eyes searched for his dear Cecilia. But Cecilia, hanging on Leonardo's arm, had disappeared, heading for the darkest corner of the hall.

Part Three

THE WHITES AND THE BLACKS

Chapter XIV

ISABEL ILINCHETA

The stentorian snores the Gamboa family broadcast often stampeded all the animals in the vicinity, and occasionally hundreds of slaves would join them—but these were immediately captured and exterminated by Tondá. Today the snores were interrupted by the arrival of an ancient and enormous coach, whose muddied wheels spattered filth over the facade of the house.

The old black coachman opened the carriage door and instantly Isabel Ilincheta, followed by her father, don Pedro, stepped down. They had come from their estate in Pinar del Río, the coffee plantation El Lucero, and they would remain only one day in Havana, enough time for Isabel to buy her Christmas and New Year's gowns. Following their usual custom on these trips to the capital, Isabel and her father would stop over with the Gambos, with whom they had links both of friendship and of mutual interest: The Ilincheta coffee plantation was right next to La Tinaja, don Cándido's property. Besides, many years before, the Ilinchetas and Gambos had arranged the future marriage of Leonardo and Isabel, and even though the couple had not in fact formalized their engagement, both don Cándido and, it seemed, don Pedro were convinced that the marriage was a certainty. In any case, thought don Cándido, we'll make sure it is.

Isabel Ilincheta was a tall young lady, robust but awkward, yellow both of hair and skin, with long arms and extremely long fingers she fluttered in all directions as she inventoried every object that came into her field of vision. This habit of hers, which her father and future father-in-law praised to the skies, she had raised to a state of perfection when she learned that as her father's only child she would have to administer the coffee plantation El Lucero, a task she carried out marvelously well. She had small eyes, virtually no eyebrows, and

44

the feminine down just above the lips she usually kept tightly shut was actually a bushy mustache.

Don Pedro walked to the center of the Gamboa dining room and was about to order the servants to announce his and his daughter's arrival when she stopped him and reproached him in a cold, sure voice.

"Papa," said the young lady, "anyone of average intelligence knows that the distance from the outer court to the center of the dining room where you are now standing is exactly twenty-five yards. If we assume that a man of your age normally covers one and a half feet with each step, we must conclude that you shouldn't have taken more than fifty paces. Well, I've calculated, accurately of course, that you took fifty-three steps. An unnecessary waste of energy. . . ."

"Quite right, daughter," humbly answered the father, who both admired and feared her. He was still expressing his regret when doña Rosa appeared, coming down the stairs, wrapped in a long robe of yellow silk and wearing felt slippers that suffocated her. Don Pedro turned toward her and, carefully measuring his footsteps, approached his hostess.

Miss Isabel did not emulate her father, at least at first, because she stayed near the coach at the outer court, watching over the provisions, the luggage, and the gifts they had brought from the estate. All the boxes (some filled with birds, others with eggs, others with animals) were opened under the expectant gaze of the young lady, who rummaged through them, counted things, and then checked over a long list she kept stuck between her breasts. Seeing at last that nothing was missing, she smilingly approached doña Rosa. Now the formalities began:

Doña Rosa: "How are things on the coffee plantation?"

Don Pedro: "Terrible, terrible. Two newly hatched chicks just died—"

Isabel: (interrupting) "Not two, father, three."

Doña Rosa: "What a disaster! Doubtless the fault of these careless blacks. Those dogs . . ."

Don Pedro: "They're ruining us, the lazy swine are ruining us. And to think we even have to feed them. Ten ounces of gold is what I've squandered buying fatback for those thankless creatures."

"What are you saying, father?" Isabel snapped furiously. "Eleven ounces and a *duro* was what we spent!"

"Quite right, child," replied her father calmly. Doña Rosa could barely believe her ears and kept saying to herself, What a woman! Perhaps this is just what Leonardito needs, since I can't be the lucky girl myself. . . . Although, who knows? . . .

Then doña Rosa asked: "Will you be here long?"

"My dear," answered Isabel, "we shall be with you only twenty-four hours, twenty-five minutes, and one second. I have calculated, exactly as I think, that by spending just that amount of time here, we shall be able to arrive at the coffee plantation just in time to oversee the inventory of dry coffee beans. As you know, they have to be counted individually several times, because those blacks are perfectly capable of hiding them, even under their tongues, and then selling our property."

"Don't I know all about it!" doña Rosa seconded her. "They've brought us almost to the brink of ruin!"

"Ruin!" exclaimed Isabel, terrified.

"Don't exaggerate, wife," said a smiling don Cándido, who at that moment was descending the stairs, followed by his favorite daughter, Carmen. Soon the other Gamboas were greeting the visitors, except for Leonardo, who was still sleeping. Don Cándido, in a powerful voice, ordered an adolescent black, Toto, who was Leonardo's lackey, to wake him up.

In the twinkling of an eye, the black was up in the young master's suite. He came back down even more quickly, even though he was dead: He landed right in the center of the hall where everyone was animatedly chatting as they sipped their afternoon chocolate.

"Oh, that Leonardo!" complained doña Rosa in mock exasperation as she contemplated the black boy's cadaver. "He's always in such a bad mood when he first wakes up." It was true: Leonardo had killed several of the slaves who awakened him, even though the order had come, as always, from don Cándido.

"Don't think that's one of his better qualities," don Cándido, visibly upset, barked at doña Rosa. "I've lost some of my best servants that way. And you know very well," he said now to don Pedro and Isabel, "that those dogs the English grow more stubborn every day about letting us unload sacks of African coal."

Gesturing, don Cándido ordered the other servants to carry Toto's body out.

"You're telling me!" interjected don Pedro, stepping aside so the dead black could be withdrawn. "I made my entire fortune thanks to my association with Pedro Blanco, my namesake. Those were other times. Nowadays it's risky business bringing loads in from Africa."

"You said it!" don Cándido seconded him. "I've got my heart in my mouth right now. The sloop *La Veloz* I sent to Guinea three months ago should already be here. It may be that those diabolic Brits have captured it."

"Don Pedro Blanco always said the same thing. In the 'business,' you've got to move quickly because there's too much envy and ill will."

"And where is that fellow?" inquired don Cándido, who had always been fascinated by the figure of Pedro Blanco.

"After the English prohibited the coal traffic, he moved to Brazil, where he married about a hundred Negresses all at the same time. Now he manufactures his own blacks and sells them at a high price."

"Not a bad business." Don Cándido laughed.

"Good heavens, Gamboa!" moralized doña Rosa. "What will the young ladies say?"

"Mama," Carmen shouted at that moment, "it's just about time for our ride. Order Dolores Aponte to hitch up the horse."

"Yes, yes," applauded Antonio. "Remember what Tita Montalvo told us—that her aunt the countess of Merlín would be at the Prado today."

"The one they call 'the Frenchwoman'?" asked Isabel rather nervously.

"The very one," answered Antonia. "They say she's got the most beautiful hair in the world."

"Then I'll wake up Leonardo," said Adela, the youngest of don Cándido's daughters, the one for whom Leonardo held a very special tenderness. "His friend, count O'Reilly, promised to introduce us to the countess."

And raising her long skirt with both hands, Adela trotted up the stairs at top speed.

"Be careful, daughter!" shouted doña Rosa.

But Adela had already entered the young man's bedroom and closed the door behind her.

Chapter XV

A COACH RIDE

At exactly 4:00 P.M., according to the enormous watch hanging on Isabel's formidable bosom, the four young ladies sallied forth in the regal coach. Bringing up the rear in a smaller open coach came Leonardo and Ernesto O'Reilly, who was showing off the impressive cross of the Order of Calatrava in his jacket lapel.

The ride began on La Muralla street, where the two vehicles stopped at the most luxurious shops so that the young ladies could make some New Year's purchases without stepping down. As they proceeded down the street they became entangled in the traffic that usually clogged this, the most commercial street in the colonial capital. Heavy carts pulled by oxen loaded with sugar, coffee, bacon, wines, and a thousand other products moved up the street in the opposite direction. All these things had their odors which, mixed with the smells of animals and excrement, disgusted the ever-so-refined ladies, who fluttered their fans in a vain attempt to blow away the stench.

As if all this were nothing, a chaise driven badly by a young coachman struck the side of the coach carrying the gentlemen. Instantly the two drivers began to argue ferociously, mixing half-Spanish and African words that began to echo along the already congested street. The cries of the ladies and the orders to proceed of the gentlemen were in vain. The black drivers finally stepped down to the street and began a duel to the death—both pulled out long knives they'd hidden in their shirts.

The confusion in the center of La Muralla street was so great that traffic all along it was paralyzed. The young ladies furiously waved their fans. Leonardo struck out blindly with his walking stick. The public, standing up in coaches, hanging over balconies, or standing in the street itself, was shouting "Hurray!" or "Boo!" Finally chance resolved the predicament, and the two battlers both fell dead at the same moment. The ladies and gentlemen could continue their ride.

Isabel Ilincheta, for security's sake, drove the coach herself and imitated the driver by straddling (we must confess) one of the horses. Count O'Reilly drove the other. But, when they reached the Puerta de la Tenaza, one of the five gates that led by drawbridge to the area beyond the walls, they found a multitude of blacks, mulattoes, whites, and even extremely elegant ladies crowded against the railing, looking toward the ditch.

Below, in the moat, the mulatto Polanco and the black Tondá, completely naked, were engaged in a kicking bout. The two celebrated swimmers, naked as the day they were born or as they dressed in their native land, dove under water, spun about, and resurfaced trying to hurt each other with tremendous kicks. This kind of fighting was called a "crocodile duel," and usually one of the contenders perished in the murky waters. Whether it was to follow the fighting or to see the naked bodies of the athletes, the fact is that the young ladies descended from their coach, a truly unusual sight in those days. Leaning dangerously far over the railing on the bridge, they observed carefully. The gentlemen also joined the crowd, either to guard the ladies or because they, too, were curious.

Finally Isabel Ilincheta looked at her huge watch and shouted: "It's five o'clock! Are we going to miss seeing the countess because of these two blacks?" And once again the company—despite Carmen Gamboa's energetic protest—began moving.

Chapter XVI

PASEO DEL PRADO

When the misses Gamboa and their company reached the Paseo del Prado, they found all of Havana society there, showing off and in a high state of expectation. The famous countess had not yet made her entrance.

Paseo del Prado—an inferior copy of the original in Madrid—was made up of a wide boulevard bordered by large trees along which the coaches paraded. There were also two cross streets so pedestrians could pass through, these generally people of lower social class but white nonetheless.

At either end of the boulevard, that is, at one end the ditch where the Botanical Gardens began and at the other the Fountain of the Lions, the lieutenant of dragoons had stationed soldiers to keep the traffic under control and to discourage speeding. Once anyone, on horseback or in a coach, entered the Paseo, he could not stop. The captain general himself had promulgated that order so that people would keep moving, and the lieutenant was charged with carrying it out.

There were so many coaches that don Cándido's daughters could coquettishly greet all their friends, those that passed by in their various vehicles and even those walking on the cross streets, almost all of these latter Spaniards employed by the public works department or other agencies of little importance.

The gentlemen, in their light two-wheeled carriages or mounted on their spirited steeds, wearing long silk stockings (so they could show off their legs), tight trousers, swallowtail coats, and top hats (that were constantly knocked off by tree branches), took advantage of the slow pace at which everything moved to strike up tantalizing conversations with the ladies. These, by waving their fans one way or another, would signal, in that unbelievably complicated and subtle language, whether they accepted the courting of the man in question.

The count of Santa Clara, the marquis of Lombillo, the duke of Villa Alta, the grandsons of the aged dowager Pérez-Crespo, the Gamez boys, and numerous other young men chatted with the Gamboa daughters. The young ladies waved their fans in all directions, at times actually slapping Isabel Ilincheta in the face. In her usual pragmatic style, she passed off the redness the fans caused as a blush caused by Leonardo's romantic—more or less—conversation.

Behind the gentlemen came a team of black slaves whose job it was to pick up hats or any other object their masters might drop.

Suddenly the crowd, which had spent hours parading back and forth under the sun, which was still blistering in the late afternoon, fell silent. Through the gate in the city wall called La Punta entered a luxurious carriage emblazoned with the arms of Montalvo: madam María de las Mercedes de Santa Cruz, countess of Merlín, had arrived at the Prado.

Perhaps because the skirt the countess was wearing was of such gigantic proportions, no one rode in the coach with her. In addition to her voluminous skirt, which would often cover both the driver and the horse when the wind lifted it, the distinguished lady wore shining boots of gold-studded felt, a tailored jacket whose sleeves were immensely wide at the wrist, as well as long violet, blue, and red ribbons that hung from her collar and spread in all directions. The glitter and color of several necklaces emphasized the whiteness of her still-firm breasts, which were practically bare because of the huge shawl the clever countess had gracefully let slip. She wore a colossal hat with an extremely high crown and an even more disproportionately wide brim. But if her figure, her costume, and her jewels were impressive, even more fascinating was her huge mane of black hair that cascaded out of her hat over her shoulders and covered the rear of the carriage. At the center of this extraordinary hair there glittered an extraordinary comb set with diamonds.

Finally, on her lap, bowing thousands of times, there was a young female monkey from southern Madagascar, dressed in French costume, a silver bell around its neck, and a gold chain the countess held in her finely gloved hand as she gracefully waved her monumental peacock-feather fan. And on they went, the countess always smiling but without looking at anyone, and the elegant monkey greeting everyone.

All those present, whether in carriages or on foot, oohed and aahed in fascination. The countess had clearly captivated Havana society, from the low-level government workers who stood openmouthed on the public walkway to the grand aristocratic women and distinguished ladies who contemplated her, enchanted with delight.

Then a kind of competition broke out among those present to see who could get near enough to the countess to greet her. As if they had been wound up and suddenly released all at the same time, carriages of all sorts, coaches, and horses made for the center of the Prado in an attempt to be next to the Montalvo coach.

Of course, because of the narrowness of the thoroughfare, it was impossible for everyone to pay their respects to the lady at the same time, with the result that the coachmen, urged on by their mistresses, were whipped into a frenzy. Each would crash his vehicle into the coach nearest his own in order to reach a better vantage point. At the same time, the men strolling on the boulevard all flooded onto the coach path, and many of them were crushed in the process under the wheels of the carriages. And if all that weren't enough, the slaves picking up windblown hats also charged toward the center of attraction, in order to recover a gentleman's hat which had been knocked off by a falling tree an incensed dragoon had cut down with his saber in a vain attempt to impose order on that chaos.

The only personage in that bizarre battlefield who seemed to be enjoying her ride was the countess, who, with her efficient monkey in her lap, impassively fluttered her monumental fan, smiling enchantingly at a lady being gutted by the wheels of a carriage or at a slave shouting for joy because despite the total confusion he had managed to recover his master's hat.

As if the crowd of distinguished people trying to pay their respects to the countess were insufficient, the great coaches-and-six belonging to the captain general and the bishop of Havana, the only two people authorized to use such vehicles, suddenly burst onto the boulevard from the Calzada de Jesús del Monte. As soon as they appeared the dragoons, under orders from their lieutenant, instantly ceased directing traffic and began beating the passersby, so the confusion redoubled.

It was then, amidst all the swirling dust that rose in waves to cloud out the very sun, that a quick and skillful hand rose up behind the countess's coach and began to pull out her diamond-encrusted comb. It was the black Dolores Santa Cruz, who after having fallen into financial ruin years earlier had gone mad and begun wandering aimlessly through the city. For a few minutes, with all the hope and concern of Havana society concentrated on them, the Negress and the countess fought it out. But Dolores Santa Cruz, evidently more dexterous in the technique of stealing diamond combs than the countess was in keeping them in her hair, finally pulled away the prize. Not only did she get the comb, but the countess's beautiful, aristocratic hair as well: María de las Mercedes de Santa Cruz, countess of Merlín, was left sitting there in her natural state: bald as a billiard ball. New oohs and aahs, expressing disenchantment, paralyzed all those present. Dolores de Santa Cruz took advantage of their shock to escape, while the countess, leaping down from her carriage, pushed her way through the crowd in pursuit of the thief.

The two women ran for more than three miles through the petrified habaneros, the Negress spouting curses in her Guinean dialect and the countess in French and Spanish. The countess swore so strongly that when the fugitive and the pursuer passed by his coach bishop Echerre crossed himself in shock and prudently shut the window. . . . Like a shot, without dropping her prize, Dolores Santa Cruz, with the countess at her heels, ran around the statue of king Charles III several times, jumped over the Neptune fountain, flew over the two lions, and without pausing clambered over the seawall. Out of breath, she looked over her shoulder and saw one step behind her the shining bald head of the countess, who, without losing a single item in her costume, neither the monumental fan nor the hysterically chattering monkey, was just about to catch her. This was a deed certainly worthy of being recorded by history—if in fact it ever happened—because the ribs that held the countess's corsets together had already sliced right through several horses belonging to the Montalvo household.

The skillful thief lost not a moment: She stripped off what little clothing she had on, leapt, with the comb in her teeth, into the turbulent waters of the bay, and swam off toward the Castillo del Morro.

The countess paused for an instant on top of the seawall as she watched the Negress's body bobbing in the waves. Was it possible she would jump into the sea to continue the chase? It was a mad idea, really. But, in point of fact, wasn't the countess herself mad? So, without taking off or putting down anything, the aristocrat hurled herself into the bay.

It may have been the result of falling from such a height or because of the rather strong wind of the tropical afternoon, or perhaps because of the two things combined: The countess's immense skirts filled with air and turned into balloons as she fell toward the water, as did her bell-shaped sleeves and her wide-brimmed hat. In a matter of seconds, the noble lady took on the shape and nautical qualities of an enormous and powerful ship of the line: Pushed on by the wind, she left the bay and crossed the Gulf of Mexico, entering, at full sail, the Atlantic Ocean. The profusion of multicolored ribbons the lady wore contributed to the brilliance of the new ship, on top of which the Madagascar monkey ecstatically and elegantly capered about. The officers aboard an English frigate (which had just captured a slave ship) confused those ribbons with their national colors, and when they caught sight of the disheveled monkey dressed in French costume they were convinced: The queen of England *herself,* on a royal ship, had come to visit her ultramarine dominions. Without wasting a second, they gave her a twenty-five-gun salute.

Carried forward by the currents of the gulf and the sea breezes, and making masterful use of her powerful fan, the distinguished lady entered the Mediterranean Sea exactly one week later. Effortlessly and gracefully she docked in the first port she reached in her adopted country, Le Havre.

"Never again," she angrily declared to her kept lover, monsieur de Chasles, as she smoothed out her new hairpiece, "will I return to the island of Cuba!"

"What happened to you?" asked her fascinated lover.

"Someone stole my comb."

"You mean you gave it to one of your more fortunate admirers," said de Chasles, who was, or pretended to be, a jealous man.

Then the mischievous monkey nodded its head several times, as if in agreement, and, giving a shriek, hid under the countess's wide skirts before she could catch it.

Chapter XVII

THE RENDEZVOUS

The lights in the Gamboa house had all been extinguished.
Only the flames in the kitchen stove, a few glowing coals,
inked intermittently. Around the stove almost all the house-
old slaves were taking advantage of the few hours before
awn to sleep, huddled around the fire.

Anyone observing the house from a distance would think
at everyone—including the servants—was fast asleep after
ch a busy day. . . . Nevertheless, as if moved by a single
oring, all the inhabitants of the mansion, as soon as the
aves had lowered the great chandeliers down from the ceil-
g and snuffed out the candles, began to move around in their
ooms. Antonia, Adela, and Carmen slipped silently toward
e balconies of their respective rooms below which waited
r them three truly impatient Spanish officers. Then a dia-
gue began which, although expressive, was composed of
niles and hushed whispers no one else in the family could
ear.

As for Isabel, taking advantage of the moonlight (so she
ouldn't burn down the candle in her room, since she in-
nded to bring it back to the coffee plantation), she mentally
viewed the coffee-harvest accounts, genuinely alarmed by
e absence of a few coffee beans.

Doña Rosa, with muffled, nervous steps, left her room
hen she thought her husband was asleep and slowly entered
er son's room. She was going to put the new repeater watch
nder his pillow: Tomorrow, thought doña Rosa, the young
an would have a happy awakening.

But don Cándido, enraged by the flight of his black cook,
as not asleep and went out, somewhat prematurely, to the
ntrance court, where he was to meet with doña Josefa. When
e got there, he found she'd already arrived. Cecilia's grand-
other wasted no time, launching into a detailed account of

55

the relationship between her granddaughter and Leonardo—the amorous relationship between the half brother and sister. Her report alarmed don Cándido even more than she had thought it would.

Even don Pedro had taken advantage of the darkness to slip down the back stairs to the kitchen, where, mixing promises and threats, he sought to seduce a Negress fresh off the boat who understood nothing he said.

So, just when all these characters were engaged in intense but virtually mute dialogues, doña Rosa ecstatically contemplated her son Leonardo, who—completely nude—seemed to be sleeping deeply.

However, Leonardo was not even vaguely asleep. To the contrary: Just when his mother had entered his room, he was taking off his sleeping robe in order to put on his street clothes. At five sharp (when doña Josefa, in the company of doña Federica, would be on her way to early mass), Leonardo had a date with Cecilia Valdés. But there he was, snoring peacefully and suffering through this all-too-loving speech his mother was making in his honor because she thought he couldn't hear her.

"Son of my soul! My best friend! My master! My life! You are my only love! You are the only one who understands me, who loves me. You are the only person with whom I could ever live. No one will ever separate us, *ever!*"

This last word frightened the young man, because if there was anything Leonardo Gamboa sincerely desired at that moment it was not only to be separated from his mother but to flee far away from her and fall into the arms of his lover.

"No one will ever separate us, *ever!*" repeated doña Rosa, as if she had guessed her son's intentions. "Here is your little repeater watch; you'll have this one and a million more if you like. Oh, my soul mate!"

She then bent over her son, who, alarmed, didn't know whether to go on pretending to sleep or to pretend he was waking up in order to stop that strange and cloying monologue.

Just then the luxurious repeater watch, perhaps because it excited doña Rosa unconsciously squeezed it, began to ring with such a clatter that doña Rosa herself gave a shriek. Her son, naked, threw himself down the stairs, colliding, as was to be expected, with don Cándido, who raised his arms in self-defense and unknowingly gave the signal for "Give me a light!" That gesture set young Tirso, who never slept but responded to his master's every desire, into motion: He ran forward with the huge brazier overflowing with crackling coals, one of which fell on Leonardo's naked body, provoking the young gentleman to swear like a trooper and strike out blindly. He knocked poor doña Josefa right off her feet.

As soon as doña Rosa saw the Negress in don Cándido's arms (he was helping doña Josefa to her feet), she began to shout "Adulterer, bad husband, degenerate!" But don Cándido, who in the darkness was unable to identify the naked man who had run down the stairs followed by doña Rosa, shouted "Whore!" and threw his wife against the dining-room table.

When the three sisters heard that word they were petrified, thinking it could only refer to each and every one of them. They fled the embraces of their lovers and ran toward the center of the entry court, where they collided with the rest of the family who were there arguing. Doña Josefa and the three Spanish officers took that opportunity to beat a hasty retreat. Hot on their trail, as naked as a newborn babe but with blood in his eye, went the outraged Leonardo Gamboa.

"Who is that naked man?" don Cándido went on shouting in ever-increasing volume. "Catch him! Stop, thief!"

All of which caused the blacks pilfering leftover food in the kitchen to think he was shouting about them. So, with an enormous clatter of pans, they, too, ran out into the entry patio, where they collided with those already there. Meanwhile, don Pedro, when he heard the shout "Stop, thief!" also thought he had been found out (he had already taken off his clothes) and ran out into the entry patio, followed by the fresh-from-Africa Negress, who thought that was what she was supposed to do. They, too, joined the tumult, which by then had turned into a single confused mass.

At that point, Isabel Ilincheta, who watched over her father as if he were a desirable lover, snatched her enormous horsewhip and began to lash out at the human mountain, although with all the confusion and darkness it was difficult to hit the target—white or black.

Don Cándido's daughters moaned and begged forgiveness, thinking they were being punished by their father; their father moaned and protested, thinking he was being whipped by

doña Rosa; doña Rosa was moaning as well because she
thought she was being defamed and beaten by her own husband; also moaning were the black sneak thieves from the
kitchen and the new Negress, who couldn't understand why
she was being beaten and who hung on to don Pedro for dear
life, even though he was moaning as he begged clemency
from his outraged daughter. And as she went on whipping
people, Isabel moaned because she never thought her father,
her beloved father, would ever betray her with a fresh
Negress. . . . It was doña Rosa who, despite all those blows
she supposed meted out by her husband, finally pronounced
some coherent words:

"Gamboa, that naked man who ran off is no lover of mine.
He's your son, Leonardo!"

This, instead of calming don Cándido, redoubled his fury.

"My son! My son!" he howled under the constant and im-
partial rain of Isabel's whiplashes. "He must be stopped! Run
after him! Call him! Stop him! Get moving, you lead-footed
creatures! Call out all the slaves! Wake up the servants . . .
He's going to Cecilia's house! He's going to visit his lover,
who is also his— No, no it cannot be! And she is alone in the
house! This is the kind of opportunity the devil takes advantage of! I myself have erred! I should have foreseen it! Prevented it! Yes, prevented it, but how? Ah, if only I could get
my hands on him! . . . I'll break his neck! I'll ship him out on
the next navy ship! Run! Run! He must be caught before it's
too late, because if not I'm liable to kill him . . . ! You! You!
It's your fault!" he rebuked doña Rosa, who couldn't understand the reason for don Cándido's diatribe. "It's your fault
because of the way you've brought him up!"

At that moment the majordomo appeared.

"Sir," he said, removing his palm-leaf hat ceremoniously
and bowing before that human mass where don Cándido was
still bellowing, "I have bad news. Your ship La Veloz was
captured by the English and they're escorting it into port."

"How could such a thing happen?" shouted all at the same
time don Cándido, his wife, his three daughters, don Pedro,
and Isabel. They were all petrified by the report, which meant
a considerable financial loss for the family.

The battle ended right then and there. The ladies and gentlemen recovered their aplomb and, smoothing down their
hair, they marched into the dining room, where they began to

think of what they could do to recover at least a part of the captured cargo.

"Those English! Those English!" howled doña Rosa. "It's easy to see they aren't Christians!"

"Losing that shipment of blacks will be a disaster for the whole family," don Cándido lugubriously stated.

"Oh, daddy!" exclaimed miss Carmen.

And she began to pour copious tears on don Cándido's knees.

"There must be a way out," reasoned the serene Isabel Ilincheta.

"The first thing to do," grumbled Gamboa, pulling on his hat, "is to visit the captain general. As a slave dealer, he'll have to side with us."

And instantly, forgetting the adventure his son was about to embark upon with his daughter, don Cándido Gamboa strode out of the house in a huff.

Chapter XVIII

DOLORES SANTA CRUZ

Dolores, Dolores... Why are so many blacks, men and women alike, named Dolores? Perhaps—that must be it—because as slaves they had no other way to express their dolorous existence: a pain indifferent to the sexes, a pain as long as their very lives, a pain that would last as long as their name. Dolores, Dolores: When parents gave their children that name, they were already informing them, with fatal and accurate prediction, of the meaning of their existence—dolorous, dolorous.... And Dolores was her name as well, a doubtlessly well-chosen name, because dolorous had been and would be her life.

Captured in Africa like an animal, she had been sold here as if she were an animal. She was intimately familiar with the stocks, the beatings, the hunger, and the twenty-hour workday. She knew that in a world of slaves and masters it was very difficult to achieve freedom. So she set about working (not like a black slave but like a hundred black slaves) day and night in several places at once. She saved every penny she earned by selling her strength and body to the highest bidder.

At night, around the stove, where the slaves would huddle to keep warm, she observed those young and old figures all clustered together and how their bodies blindly sought each other out, trying to protect themselves, unconsciously trying to hide, always trying to rest their heads in dark places in order not to see so much horror. Thus, amidst moans and kicks, that dream, that nightmare, went on.

Thanks to her incessant work, trickery, and saving, she had purchased her freedom. But to be free and poor is to go on being a slave. She worked even harder and became the owner of several gambling houses, a bakery, and a shoemaker shop.

It was then that the lawyers appeared with thousands of papers and questions: Where are your property titles? Who ranted them to you? Where are the seals and the signatures of the superintendent and the executor? . . . And, since many of those lawyers worked for the very gentlemen who had sold her the properties and who now wanted to get them back from her, the papers never appeared. Moreover, in order to defend herself from those lawyers, she had to pay other lawyers who themselves were subordinates to or representatives of the first lawyers. With the result that one day she was officially informed that not only did her properties no longer belong to her but that she owed a fortune to the lawyers who had defended her. And if she didn't pay up with cash on the barrelhead, Dolores Santa Cruz would have to pay with her labor; that is, under the law, she would spend the rest of her life as a slave.

There were two ways in which she could escape this sentence: madness or death. She optimistically chose madness.

That's right, she feigned madness. In fact she was saner than she had ever been. She figured out how to bamboozle the judges and wandered the streets of Havana doing bizarre things and singing strange songs, half in Spanish, half in some African language. Her "Miss, miss, moose, here's D'lores Santa Cruz, I use' ta be uh queen, but duh lawyas picked me clean!" became so well known that people finally stopped paying her any attention. In that way, she could pass unnoticed, be free, and plot.

The act was that night and day, as she sang those seemingly unbalanced or naive ditties, she would meet with runaway or seditious blacks, she would burn down stables and houses, poison the masters' food, unleash plagues, poison rivers and ponds, and carry messages back and forth between groups of runaway slaves. Her "Miss, miss, moose" was often a password, which, depending on how it was pronounced, could transmit an order or serve as a warning.

They hadn't defeated her and would never be able to defeat her.

But all her sangfroid vanished that afternoon as she was pegging along the Prado and distributing switchblade knives among the seditious coachmen. She saw the countess of Merlin, who was laughing not only at the slaves but at everyone else, and all with gestures of benevolence, even of nobility. It was a hypocrisy so refined or exotic that Dolores Santa Cruz, unaccustomed to it, had no defense against it.

It was then that she walked toward the countess, not only

intending to rob her diamond comb (which she would use to pay for a shipment of English rifles) but also to yank out her hair. And that's exactly what she did. Because the countess in fact was not bald until Dolores Santa Cruz scalped her by pulling out her hair with all the accumulated fury of fifty-six years. It was at that instant, with that freshly pulled hair in her hands—although she did lament she hadn't gotten the head as well—that she felt truly liberated for the first time in her life. She had humiliated not only the countess but all those people there who tried to imitate her as well. It's true the lady was more daring than Dolores thought she would be and chased her right to the bottom of the sea.

But the Negress, swimming under water, had gone through the caves beneath the Castillo del Morro and reached the Regla district, where, surrounded by conspirators and pirates (the countess's hair draped over her own kinky curls), she was calculating the value of the diamond comb and plotting new revenge.

Chapter XIX

THE RENDEZVOUS

"Good heavens!" exclaimed Cecilia Valdés, looking up at the old clock on the wall. "It's almost five and I still haven't finished painting you up! Leonardo will be here any minute."

Cecilia was not speaking, despite appearances, to the old clock on the wall, but to her great-grandmother, doña Amalia. Cecilia, dipping her brush in a pot of white paint, was changing doña Amalia's black skin into ivory. And she went right on painting the old lady as she spoke to her.

"White! That's right! The whitest!... That's how Leonardo must see you. Leonardo must never know that you're a retouched Negress. If he were to find out, he'd never marry me. White! White! Not even mulatta!..."

The centenarian Negress unwillingly received that coat of paint, but, prostrate as she was, she could do little to protest. With great difficulty, she spread her varnish-covered lips and said in a whisper she wished were a shout:

"Cecilia, chile, ah alays been black an' ah lak it dat way. Cain't you at leas' let me die wit' my right culuh?"

"What?" exclaimed the suddenly serious great-granddaughter. "That's the limit! I turn you into a human being and that's the thanks I get? Complaints? Do you know how hard it was for me to get this barrel of white paint from the Catalonian over on Empedrado street? He charged me two ounces of gold. Did you hear me? Two ounces!"

"Ah wanna be black. Leave me mah own culuh."

The Negress, or rather the white woman, since only one of her withered breasts was still black, and that, too, would be white in a moment, again protested in a low voice.

"So you want to be black, eh? But don't you understand that in this world a black is worth less than a dog? Even if you work and get free, even if you get money—which is almost impossible. Look what happened with Dolores Santa Cruz.

63

They never forgave her for wanting to sleep in a comfortable bed like a white person, or for having her own carriage. The whites tripped her up in their white laws until they stripped her bare. If she'd been white none of that would ever have happened. . . . That's why my children are going to be white. White! No backsliding black babies for me! They're not going to go through what you and my grandmother did."

Just then the front door, which Cecilia had left ajar, opened and in walked Leonardo Gamboa.

"And how's the most beautiful mulatta in the world doing?"

"You don't love me, Leonardo. You say things like that to me because you don't love me."

"How can you say that, 'Celia my love? I risked my very life to come here. You should know that my father and his damned pack of blacks are right on my heels."

"Dat dawg know jus' whut he doin'," murmured the great-grandmother, almost expiring as she did so.

"What *is* that?" exclaimed the surprised Leonardo when he spied the freshly painted old lady, who was lying on a plank on the floor.

"Oh, *that's* nothing! Just Mimi, my great-grandmother. She's sick, that's whys she's so pale. . . . Great-grand-mammy, this is mister Gamboa, my fiancé."

"Youah fiancé? Youah fiancé? You mean youah pimp, you whoah! Who evah saw uh black girl wit' uh white fiancé?"

"She's delirious," explained the desperate Cecilia. "It's fever. She just came from Spain."

"Yes, she sure is pale," answered Leonardo Gamboa, drawn by curiosity to the shining body as he discovered the black breast Cecilia hadn't as yet painted.

Leonardo smiled in disgust but said nothing, in order not to contradict Cecilia, with whom he wanted to spend some time.

"Leonardo," said Cecilia, embracing him. "Promise you'll never leave me."

"I swear it!" he answered instantly and firmly, although that same morning he was to leave with Isabel Ilincheta to spend the holidays out in the country.

"Leonardo, dearest Leonardo, promise me you'll marry me, that you'll be my husband."

"I swear it!" he categorically announced, although within two weeks he intended to become engaged to Isabel Ilincheta.

"Oh, my love! No one will ever separate us!"

As she said this Cecilia slammed the front door and returned to her lover.

Soon the embracing couple was thrashing about on the floor.

As they lay there, illuminated only by the candle that burned under the Virgin pierced by the flaming sword, Cecilia casually picked up her brush and finished painting her great-grandmother's dried-out teat.

It was never known whether it was because of the paint or because of the blow she may have accidentally received from the lovers as they rolled about, but the fact is that Amalia Alarcón, a Negress born in Guinea, died in Cuba one hundred years later—pure white.

Chapter XX

THE CAPTAIN GENERAL

Genuinely concerned, don Cándido de Gamboa, accompanied by two other plantation owners—the slave dealers Madrazo and Meriño—took himself to the offices of the captain general in order to speak personally with the maximum authority in Cuba, don Francisco Dionisio Vives. But when he got there, he was told that the captain general was in the patio of the Castillo de la Fuerza enjoying a cockfight.

The captain general was so addicted to cockfighting that he had turned it into the national game, even turning the Castillo de la Fuerza into a gigantic cockpit. So the three men headed for the Castillo, and after identifying themselves at various checkpoints and guardpoints, they reached the central patio of the fortress.

Surrounded by the captain of the port, the bishop of Havana—Echerre, whom we've already met—assorted Spanish noble ladies, and numerous courtiers, the captain general was in rapt contemplation, almost in the very center of the pit, of a clash between two powerful cocks, which were furiously tearing each other to shreds.

Above the crowing and cackling of more than a hundred fighting cocks all waiting their turn to die, it was possible to hear the enthusiastic and at times unprintable comments of the captain general each time his favorite cock, a superb Malayan, spurred his adversary, a heavy English rooster.

The person in charge of caring for and training the cocks was, aside from being a master in this sport or game, one of the most terrible murderers in the land. His official name was Ambassador Flórez, but his nickname among the people was "Bucket of Blood." In addition to the numerous crimes and tortures he perpetrated among the lower classes under the

66

orders of the captain general, he had hanging over his head a treacherous and sinister crime against one of the great figures in the city. The dead man's family, all nobles and some of them churchmen, had sworn eternal vengeance against the killer.

But a sister of Flórez, who happened to be very beautiful, had a private chat with the captain general. The interview (which took three days and three nights), Flórez's loyalty to the captain, and, above all, his expertise in fighting cocks enabled the murderer to become the number one protégé of the captain general. In order to protect Flórez and at the same time not to lose his services as cock trainer, he had the gigantic pit built in the patio of the Castillo de la Fuerza. And that's how Flórez ended up there, safe, sound, well fed, and protected by two powers, the Castillo and the captain general himself.

All these precautions didn't keep the dead man's family from gathering every morning on the other side of the moat around the Castillo in order to methodically hurl stones against the fortress as a warning that they had not forgiven Flórez and that their thirst for justice had not been slaked. Almost all those present in the patio were prepared for these inconveniences: The bishop, instead of his customary miter, wore a steel helmet; the military officers carried enormous metal shields; the ladies, parasols which were actually made of chain mail. Even Tondá, the elegant black who was the captain general's favorite, carried, in addition to his shining and handsome sword, a kind of large metal plate which he kept at the ready to cover his protector's head.

The captain general's jubilant shouts rang out. The Malayan cock had killed the English bird with a single stroke. The entire company burst into applause. And just at that moment, as if the attackers had been waiting for just such an opportunity, the stones began to rain down.

The elegant ladies of the court, always smiling, opened their chain-mail parasols; the officers covered themselves with their shields; Tondá instantly protected the captain general with his plate; the consuls set up a kind of portable roof; and the bishop, always striving to call attention to himself, stuck a huge chromium miter with gold tassels on top of his steel helmet. Only Gamboa and his two friends ran in panic from one side of the castle to another, hit, now on the shoulders, now on the ears, now right on their heads, by those implacable stones.

The sight of them aroused both the curiosity and the laughter of the captain general, who, interrupting the delightful conversation he was carrying on with one of the grand ladies, signaled to Tondá to bring those three gentlemen before him.

Rapidly, protecting himself as best he could from those stones that seemed to rain down from heaven, Gamboa explained to His Excellency the reason for his visit. The English had captured the brigantine *La Veloz*, chock-full of blacks that hadn't come from Africa, no sir, but who were already ours, who spoke Spanish and were Christians, blacks we were bringing over from Puerto Rico. Which is why I have come before you to beg for clemency and justice. . . . And under that rain of stones, he discreetly showed the captain general, the maximum authority in the island, a purse with more than five hundred gold coins in it.

The captain general, never losing his aplomb and taking the purse with an air of indifference, said:

"Gentlemen, I recognize the injustice and damage this treaty, which concedes to England the right to search our merchant ships, causes us. But the wise ministers of His Majesty the King thought it proper to approve it, and we, loyal subjects, must obey it. . . . In vain do I try to look the other way. You just go on smuggling black packages, as you call them, through the worst places, and you never remember the poor captain general, on whom the English consul takes his revenge. Because no sooner does a sack of coal, again to use your terminology, turn up here than the consul turns up as well, venting his rage on me. . . . With regard to the shipload of blacks you've brought from Africa *and not from Puerto Rico*"—and here the captain general could not keep himself from smiling despite the fact that the rain of stones falling on the plate over his head grew heavier—"the honorable English consul has already been to see me, accompanied by the commander of the ship that captured *La Veloz*, lord Clarence Paget. Naturally I'll give a good report on you to the mixed commission which has charge of the matter. . . . But that, gentlemen, will not solve the problem. The matter can only be resolved if you show yourselves to be most friendly to the consul and the lord; so friendly that you succeed in convincing them to come to the ball the Philharmonic Society is giving at year's end. . . . That's the only way, gentlemen!" the captain general shouted above the ricocheting stones as he smiled again in a conspiratory way. "If we get the consul and the lord to come to the ball, we'll get rid of the two of them in a truly original way, by means of a species of justice we might call *absolutely royal*. So, then, invite those distinguished gentlemen to the Philharmonic ball—oh, and don't forget that they *should not wear masks*. . . . Until then, diplomacy and patience, my friends. And don't compromise the honor of your captain general any further. Remember, prudence is the first moral virtue."

Chapter XXI

FRIENDSHIP

Just as Leonardo Gamboa was leaving Cecilia's house, Nemesia Pimienta burst in.

"Cecilia!" she said excitedly. "Come on! You have to come with me to the Gamboa house!"

"What's going on?" asked Cecilia, quickly getting dressed.

"I want you to be cured once and for all of your foolish faith in men," answered the spiteful Nemesia, who was still in love with Leonardo and who still wanted to come between him and Cecilia.

Both women immediately left the San Juan de Dios alley on the run.

An enormous carriage was standing in front of the Gamboa residence. Cecilia could see that Leonardo was helping Isabel Ilincheta step into the carriage and was kissing her hand as he did so. In a flash she understood everything: The Gamboas, as was their custom, were going out to the country to celebrate Christmas and New Year and Leonardo was going with them, above all, with Isabel.

The mulatta's self-control dissolved as she approached the carriage. Leonardo had just rested one foot on the step when Cecilia struck him—so hard that he tumbled headfirst right over one of the wheels. Surprised, Isabel poked her head out of the window.

"Adela! What have you done?" she shouted, mistaking Cecilia for the youngest of the Gamboa girls, an easy error to make because they looked so much alike.

But she was quickly disabused because Cecilia, snarling out "Whore!" slapped her with such violence that the lady from Pinar del Río fell backwards onto the seat.

The ladies and gentlemen of the neighborhood, peering out their windows, were all expecting to see the carriage curtains part and a white handkerchief appear to wave "a fond farewell." Even the pedigreed dogs, trained for such events, were left standing on their hind legs. Then Isabel Ilincheta, vaulting onto one of the carriage horses, thundered after Cecilia and Nemesia in order to crush them under the wheels. Those who remained inside the carriage also had good reason to fear for their lives. . . .

As the two frightened mulattas ran, every single door behind which they might have sought asylum slammed shut in their faces.

"A fire!" some shouted from their balconies.

"Some runaway slaves are rioting!" declared others.

"It's the English pirates again!" was the decision of the majority.

Cecilia Valdés and Nemesia Pimienta continued to run through the city, knocking down omelet stands, stoves filled with hot coals, gaming tables where people were playing with dice and cards, and carts loaded with imported sweets. The pursued and the pursuers smashed through the slaughterhouse for hogs (to the joy of the condemned swine—which, emitting operatic grunts of jubilation, overran palaces and shops), they dissolved a religious procession, a slave auction, the entire market day in the Plaza Vieja, and, finally, a company carrying a caged woman—an adultress and murderer—to the gallows. She made her getaway along with the other two women as the entire company—the soldiers, nuns, and the hangman—joined the pursuers.

"Stop the murderers! Stop them!" the blacks, mulattoes, craftsmen, Spaniards, criollos, children, and pimps were all shouting as they watched the three women hotly pursued by a most varied train headed by Isabel Ilincheta.

But the lady who had been condemned to death (instead of merely being threatened by it, as were Nemesia and Cecilia) smashed open the door of the Church of the Holy Spirit and burst in begging asylum and clemency from father Gaztelu. . . . The three women finally found protection in that place which by law could not be violated by the authorities.

Numerous political conspirators, runaway slaves, and even common criminals were already there. When they saw the three fugitives, all of them beautiful, they broke into excited applause and made room for them.

While the crowd outside roared and threatened to tear down the church, Isabel Ilincheta squinted at the huge clock she always had hanging around her neck. Seeing that it was almost time for her to be home on the coffee plantation to count the slaves, she spurred the horse: The coach and all those in it, the ladies and gentlemen of the Gamboa household and Isabel's highly alarmed father, passed through the Tenaza Gate like a shot and were lost in a cloud of dust that clattered toward the estate El Lucero.

Chapter XXII

ON LOVE

A love, a great love.... That's what it had to be—and that's what it was: Cecilia's love for Leonardo. Not a momentary passion, not a passing fancy, but an absolute fusion. A challenge and a flying in the face of convention. A triumph over her early life, over her dark, doubtlessly sinister past, over her useless present, and over her horrifying future, which, following laws and mores, was already determined.

Because a love, a great love, had to be, above all, a victory, a higher state, something that would exceed her fondest desires. A great love had to be—she said to herself, she intuited, she thought—a flight toward something we secretly know does exist and that waits out there to complete us, so that we finally may be ourselves. Something without which no life would be bearable.... A great love, then, should be a flight. She could not conceive that a passion so sublime could exist and grow in the limited framework of the world of misery in which she had always lived. Ah, a great love was, had to be for her, a legend made real: the enchanted prince, the earthly god impassioned and charmed, the superior man, handsome and strong, intent on taking her and with a virile gesture (itself a supreme pleasure) transporting her far away. Far from that foul alley, far from those narrow, damp, and dark rooms surrounded by grotesque, prying eyes; far from that asphyxiating world controlled by old crones who turned any small pleasure—the only kind they'd ever have—into a perennial motive for repentance.... No, she would never be like her grandmother or her great-grandmother, mocked women who took refuge in a pious but implacable piety.

Beyond the San Juan de Dios alley with its incessant chatter and the cries of the Negresses hawking their wares, with its dusty or mud-spattered facades, was Angel Hill. The luxurious church dominated everything in sight, and at its feet

73

*were the salons, palaces, theaters, boulevards, carriages,
and shops: the world, the real world, to which she, they,
could not gain access. To enter into it like a grande dame,
through the door of honor, accompanied by the ringing of
bells—that, too, was her goal. She would be the lady
escorted by her vanquished lover, the woman who, surrounded by jealousy and jewelry, would flaunt the victory of
her beauty and her love in the face of the thousand laws,
prejudices, sinister traditions, and powerful interests opposed
to her marriage to Leonardo.*

*Even when she was a child, Cecilia Valdés would climb the
steep stairs of Angel Hill, hide among the church columns,
and contemplate the magnificent weddings high Havana society would celebrate there because it was the most luxurious
and highest place in the city. No man or woman of color could
be married in that place. There such ceremonies were re-
served for whites only and only for the most powerful among
them. But Cecilia, because she was Leonardo Gamboa's
bride-to-be, would demand that her wedding be celebrated in
that church. The most prestigious, most sacred, the loftiest
place in the city would be the battleground where she would
shout her challenge.*

*Splendidly attired in white, she would march to the altar,
and all those present would have to bow as she passed and
greet her with polite reverence while she, on Leonardo's arm,
would grant them an ironic smile. She would march down the
aisle knowing that with each step she took centuries of scorn
and injustice were being mocked. . . . Yes, because a great
love for her was a great vengeance and an absolute
liberation. . . . But it was also a secret, sweet, and inexplic-
able meeting with her own best self.*

Part Four

A TRIP TO
THE COUNTRY

Chapter XXIII

AT THE COFFEE PLANTATION

The company arrived safe and sound at the Ilincheta estate, whose fences were completely covered with tiny white bells and perfumed tropical flowers that only bloom at Christmas. Millions of bees supplemented the whiteness with gold and music.

The first to alight from the coach was Leonardo, who wanted to help Isabel since—under express orders from don Cándido—he was to court her. But Isabel couldn't waste her time on gallantry. Quickly jumping off the horse, she ran to the center of the main patio, loudly rang a huge bell hanging there, and summoned all the slaves in an instant. She then counted each and every one.

The overseer, a man of fearful aspect named Blás, received and transmitted Isabel's orders.

"Put 'em to work!" said the young lady.

And the overseer, whip in hand, set all the slaves in motion.

"Isabel," whispered Leonardo in her ear in honeyed tones, "you are really the girl of my dreams . . ."

"Blás," said the impassive and authoritarian Isabel, "haven't you washed the horse yet?"

Instantly she ran to where the horse just washed by the overseer was standing. Lifting one of its hooves, she confirmed that its shoes were much too worn. The fearful overseer bent over behind the young lady while Leonardo persisted in his lovemaking.

"Isabel, Isabel, I never imagined a woman could be so perfect. . . ."

"Blás!" shouted Isabel to the overseer, who was standing

ight behind her. "Remind the slaves that they may only play he drum on Christmas and after six in the afternoon."

"Yes, missy," answered the fearful and fearsome overseer.

Leonardo was about to take the young lady by the arm, but at that moment she ran toward the well, where various slaves were drawing up a barrel of water.

"Blás, how's the water level in the well?"

"Good, missy, real good!" optimistically affirmed the overseer.

"Let's see," said Isabel.

And, taking hold of the rope the slaves were using, she measured the level of the well water as well as the total depth of the well itself. Then she made a grimace of disgust. Evidently the well did not have as much water as she had hoped.

"Blás!" she shouted in her tranquil way. "From now on you'll give less water to the blacks and animals. . . . By the way, I only see two of the three turtles I put down there last week to purify the water."

"The other one must be swimming down near the bottom," said Blás, trembling.

"It's possible." Isabel meditated briefly. "In any case, we'd better find out. Bring me the ladder."

The overseer and some slaves immediately fetched a long rope ladder, and Isabel, periodically grabbing on to the plants that grew on the sides of the wall, scrambled down to the lower depths.

The slaves and the overseer peered over the top, all fearful, not about the danger Isabel's life might be in but about the danger their lives were certainly in: If the turtle was missing, they were doomed. Isabel reached the water, dove in, found the turtle resting on the bottom, surfaced, and climbed out. Then she continued her inspection. With a velocity and discipline that were really admirable, she counted—with Blás and Leonardo at her heels—all the coffee bushes one by one and all the ripening coffee beans. Then she counted the beans drying and made a general accounting—all the while counting the Cape jasmines, which were just opening their pearly blossoms, each plant in the garden, and each fruit or vegetable on every one. Then she took her basket and gathered up the eggs the hens had laid while she was away. She made a census of pigs, birds, sheep, and of domestic animals, and opening up the beehives she counted each and every honeycomb, as well

as the workers and drones (these latter she crushed betwee
her fingers). Finally, at midday, with her basket filled wi
eggs, she lay down on the soft clover to take her brief an
scheduled rest. That was the opportunity Leonardo was awai
ing to make his amorous confession. In the distance, the crie
or songs of the slaves echoed. Above, numerous guinea hen
crossed the skies.

"Isabel," said the young Gamboa, "for a long time no
I've wanted to confess my love for you. I wish you woul
become my bride. You contain, really, all the virtues. . . ."

"One's missing!" shouted Isabel, truly desperate.

"Which one?" said Leonardo, intrigued and surprised b
the girl's frankness.

"The spotted one! The spotted guinea hen!" exclaimed Isa
bel, immediately standing up. "I counted all of them as the
were flying over us! There should be one thousand si
hundred and six guinea hens, and I've only counted one thou
sand six hundred and five! Yes, the spotted hen is the on
missing! Some black must have eaten her up! Just wait till
get my hands on him! Just wait! Blás! Blás!"

In under a minute numerous squads of blacks and trackin
dogs were moving in every direction on the extensive coffe
plantation, intent on capturing—dead or alive—the guine
hen thief. That hen laid more eggs, according to Isabel, tha
any other guinea hen on the estate.

The uproar caused by the search for the bird and its thie
was so huge that Leonardo Gamboa left off making his form
declaration to Isabel for the rest of the day.

"Forget about it until we're at our plantation," do
Cándido said in the hall. "There she won't have so man
distractions." And, contemplating the groups of dogs an
blacks which, led by Isabel and armed to the teeth, wer
shaking all the bushes, don Cándido exclaimed, "She really
an extraordinary woman!"

Chapter XXIV

THE STEAM ENGINE

Like a cannonball, the swift, fiery sun fell behind the immense palm grove just beyond the mansion as the owners of the Tinaja sugar plantation, accompanied by their family, friends, and employees, filed into the shed where the sugarcane juice was boiled down.

The priest from El Mariel led the procession, dressed up in his best cassock and his ceremonial bonnet. Behind came doña Rosa, her three daughters, and Isabel Ilincheta, all wearing long dresses, overskirts, and mantillas, each one bearing a long wax taper. Bringing up the rear, solemn in their black frock coats, came don Cándido de Gamboa, Leonardo, the technician from the United States, the plantation doctor, the overseer, and the sugarboy (or master). They carried their hats under their arms.

The ceremony about to take place was of the highest importance. For the first time in that mill—and, for that matter, in the whole of Cuba—a steam engine was going to be used to grind sugarcane. This meant that the old grinding machines powered by horses or mules, sometimes by the slaves themselves, would be rendered obsolete, opening the way for a much more efficient and profitable production system.

The enormous machine, manufactured in England but brought to Cuba from the United States, had been erected out in the open, right in the center of the plant, next to the boiling-down shed, where a multitude of barefoot and half-naked slaves rushed to and fro, kept moving by the overseer's whip.

In the twinkling of an eye, the servants set up comfortable wood and wicker armchairs on one side of the machine, where the ladies and gentlemen, after having placed their candles around the engine, sat down to observe the ceremony.

Wine and cigars, liberally dispensed by don Cándido, circulated among the gentlemen, while the ladies drank hot sugarcane juice laced with Canary Islands brandy. All this was ceremoniously served out by the sugarboy, a handsome young Creole who was clearly courting Adela. The mere sight of this threw her brother Leonardo into a rage because he could not conceive of Adela's loving any man—except, of course, himself.

Meanwhile, the slaves, under the incessant whip, threw wood into the furnaces in order to raise the temperature in the boiler so that the mechanical grinder could begin to work.

When the Yankee technician had calculated that the pressure was high enough, the priest stood up, walked toward the colossal engine, muttered a brief prayer in Latin, and sprayed holy water on the cylinders from a silver hyssop. Immediately two gentlemen carried over a bale of sugarcane which the four young ladies had bound up in white, blue, and red silk ribbons.

The men deposited the sugarcane in the machine. The priest made the sign of the cross, and the others followed suit. The first machine-operated sugar grinding ever to take place on the celebrated Tinaja plantation was about to occur. Everyone, even the slaves, was in a high state of expectation. But the grinder refused to budge.

The Yankee technician checked the pressure on the boiler gauges. The slaves were ordered to throw more wood into the furnaces. The gauges registered even higher pressure. But the grinder remained paralyzed. Another touch of the whip made the blacks feed those fiery mouths at a dizzying pace. The pressure reached the danger point. At any moment the belts would begin to move and the grinders would begin to grind.

But nothing happened.

Don Cándido looked desperate, doña Rosa fidgeted about in her wide armchair, the priest began a prayer, gazing all the while at the clear sky of the tropical evening.

"Maybe some belt or rod or something in the machinery is blocked." The sugarboy translated what the Yankee technician was saying.

"Well, unblock it, then!" roared don Cándido.

The technician, the overseer, the sugarboy, even the plantation doctor himself (stethoscope at the ready) approached the boiler to try to find the problem. But the huge machine was red-hot, and they were obliged to retreat.

"Call the least stupid blacks!" the overseer ordered. "And tell 'em to get up there and see if any of the belts are off track!"

Instantly several blacks, all young and strong, climbed up onto the machinery under a rain of whiplashes and death threats. While their feet and hands fried they had to scamper around as best they could over that blazing surface. Finally one of them, thinking, no doubt, that he'd found the source of the blockage, opened the boiler's enormous safety valve. There was a strange explosion, and the black, thrown by the force of the compressed steam and trailing clouds of smoke behind him, flew into the air, rising to such an altitude that he sailed out of sight beyond the horizon. Another cannonade resounded, and a second black flashed across the sky. A third discharge, and yet another black faded into the blue.

Don Cándido, scared out of his wits, got up, waving his arms around and shouting:

"Stop that machine, or all my slaves will disappear! I should have known you can't do business with the English! That's no steam engine, it's an English trick to send the blacks back to Africa!"

No sooner had the blacks heard that revelation than they ran toward the machine. In less than a minute hundreds of them had scrambled barefoot onto the gigantic, red-hot back of the metal beast shouting "Back to Guinea!" They were jumping right into the pipe covered by the safety valve, and immediately zooming, often dozens at a time, over the horizon.

With an unheard-of speed, almost all the slaves on that work shift got ready for a trip they all believed would be a long one. Among the innumerable blacks who dove into the machine, a few had hastily gathered up and taken along such belongings as they had: a gigantic gourd, some coconuts, a live *jutía* that squeaked in rage like a giant rat, primitive trunks filled with partially carved stones or wooden idols, and, most of all, drums of various sizes.

Dressed in their finest—red or blue rags—they all plunged into the escape pipe, and then, once in the air, inflamed no doubt by their euphoria and the pleasure of thinking that they were finally flying home, they sang and danced with such color, rhythm, and movement that it was a genuinely celestial spectacle—both literally and figuratively.... Of course, the fact that they were flying greatly enhanced their lightness and grace, and allowed them to accomplish twirls, jetés, pirouettes, and do-si-dos that were much more syncopated and daring than what they could have done on the ground. So high up, their songs and the *tam-tam* of their instruments achieved such diaphanous sonority that they shook the very clouds with their frenetic echoes.

Scattered over the unchanging azure, the slaves executed (inter alia) splendid Yoruba and Bantu (Congo and Lucumí) songs and dances to give thanks to Shangó, Ochún, Yemayá, Obatalá, and other African deities. At the same time, a massive full moon (an accomplice, or so it seemed, of the fugitives) appeared. The open flower of the night, shining and gigantic, silhouetted the small convulsive black dots that disappeared into the stratosphere at top speed, as if a desperate intuition made them seek in another world what they had never found in this one.

Meanwhile, down on earth, the Gamboa family and their associates were in total panic, despite this fascinating spectacle without precedent in the entire history of dance—a fact the anthropologist Lydia Cabrera verified in her classical essay "Let the Boogie Begin." The blacks continued to climb the machine and fly through the skies.

Don Cándido, the priest, and several of the gentlemen tried to stem that tide as best they could, but the wild machine kept on catapulting blacks. Finally it seemed stuffed, both by the number of bodies that dove at the same time into its belly and by the constant pressure of the fire and steam: It slipped off its base and began to spin uncontrollably around the plantation, shooting off slaves in every direction.

The terrified ladies and even the gentlemen ran, often chased by the machine, which, vomiting fire and blacks, spun, immersed in an enormous cloud of smoke, creating a clamor that grew more and more stentorian.

"High treason!" exclaimed don Cándido. "Call out the army! Bring out the guns!"

By midnight, when the troops arrived and succeeded in shooting the infernal steam engine to pieces, thousands of blacks had flown over the huge plantation, smashing into mountains, hills, and palm trees, and even crashing on the distant beach.

The slaves who stayed behind—without don Cándido's permission—played the drums that night in honor of those brave souls who had flown back to Africa.

Chapter XXV

ROMANCE UNDER THE PALM TREES

Walking hand in hand, Isabel and Leonardo stroll through the immense palm grove near the Gamboa mansion. Isabel's white dress, lace sleeves and trailing bows, sweeps the path with its long train. It was a chore Isabel assigned herself when she saw how full of trash those lanes were. Even as I stroll I do some useful work, thought the young lady. After all, when I'm married to Leonardo, this will be my property too.

And as she went along thinking these thoughts she simultaneously—also to save time—commented on the disaster which had occurred the day before with the steam engine. "Really, everything happened in less than it takes to say an Our Father." She put special emphasis on the "Our Father" to show Leonardo just how deep her religious sentiments ran and, once more, to save time: Tonight, she thought, when I say my prayers I won't have to say "Our Father" because I've already said it.

But the loss of two thousand five hundred (the precise number lost, according to Isabel) blacks mattered little to Leonardo because the estate was overflowing with blacks and because, as his father always said, they could always get more from Africa when the supply ran low. Leonardo was worried because he still had not formally asked Isabel to marry him, and every day don Cándido pressed and urged him to get it over with. And as soon as Leonardo married Isabel, don Cándido would transfer the title of Count of the House of Gamboa (requested and paid for many years before) to him. As he thought about the title he lusted after, the young man squeezed the young lady's hand and discreetly proposed they plunge into the heart of the palm grove. And Isabel, always thinking about sweeping that area, willingly accepted.

They hadn't gone very far when an unbearable stench stopped them. Suddenly a flock of scabby vultures, owls, and hawks fluttered into the air and revealed the already rotten body of a black. Holding her breath, Isabel examined the cadaver, already deprived of eyes and intestines. "Here we have a case," she explained to Leonardo, "of mechanical asphyxiation."

"Of what?" asked Leonardo, intrigued.

"This man killed himself by swallowing his own tongue."

The very idea seemed to disconcert the young man.

"When a black is in despair or doesn't want to work anymore," went on the young lady, taking on professorial airs, "that is, when he no longer wants to go on living and has no lethal weapons nearby (you know we don't allow it), he pulls his tongue violently and then bends it back and pushes it down his throat. It stops up his throat and asphyxiates him. If we were to do an autopsy on this body, we would see that the liver, the lungs, and the brain have a very dark color because of the blood. . . . But let's be on our way: The stench is overwhelming."

Walking swiftly and still holding hands, they went more deeply into the solitary grove, where the only noise came from the rustle of the leaves of the majestic palms. But once again the intense, unbearable stink of a body in an advanced state of decomposition assaulted their noses.

"This one," Isabel said, making her way through the carrion birds and other creatures and pointing at the dead man, "killed himself by pitilessly smashing his head with the very iron ball he has chained to his ankle."

"You're absolutely right," said Leonardo, peering at the battered skull. "But let's find a more pleasant spot."

And without a second thought he clasped Isabel's hand once again. They had barely gone on a few paces when they came upon yet another corpse, also topped with the same birds and beasts.

"This one," explained Isabel, impassive in the face of the rage of scabby vultures, hawks, and other creatures whose banquet she was interrupting, "killed himself with his own hands. Look, his fingers are still wrapped around his throat."

"How unbelievably selfish," remarked Leonardo. "He could have chosen a more remote spot."

And, gently tugging on the young lady's arm, he led her

toward the shade of a tall royal palm. They were just getting ready to sit down in that cool spot when from the top of that high tree plummeted the cadaver of a black which smashed right at the feet of our strolling lovers.

"This one," explained the ever-serene Isabel, "was one of the slaves shot into the sky yesterday by the steam engine. He fell on top of this tree and stayed there until just now, when the wind or some other natural phenomenon shook him loose."

Then they both looked up and saw a totally unprecedented sight: From the top of every tree in the grove, as far as they could see in all directions, there hung one or more black cadavers.

"And they thought they were flying back to Africa," commented Leonardo scornfully.

He again tugged on Isabel's sleeve and led her to the shade of yet another palm, but instantly not one but three bodies fell at their feet, obliging them to move on.

Attracted by a strange noise, the young couple stopped and looked back. Thousands of scabby vultures, hawks, owls, mice, snakes, rats, slugs, worms, cockroaches, flies, and even packs of wild dogs were following them. Leonardo and Isabel began to walk at a brisker pace, but all the members of that strange company, slithering, hopping, or flying, also quickened the pace.

"No doubt," expounded Isabel, looking at the extraordinary army drawing ever closer to them, "they've noticed that every time we stop somewhere a cadaver appears, and they've concluded that if they keep following us they'll always be assured of a full stomach. Keep walking and pretend you don't notice them," she whispered to Leonardo, who, when he saw the sinister train behind him, almost fainted dead away.

Leonardo and Isabel started walking again, quite briskly, but always feigning indifference, thinking they would thus confuse their voracious followers. But every time they passed beneath a palm tree (and there were thousands), the tree would shake (because of Isabel's wide skirt) and a dead slave would fall at their feet. The beasts would instantly devour the cadaver and then go on—even stronger, more excited, and greedier—following the couple.

Tracing a huge circle, Isabel and Leonardo advanced

through the entire palm grove at a truly high rate of speed, always gaining some ground on their pursuers every time a black fell from above. When they reached open ground they began to run toward the mansion, shouting at the top of their lungs as they did so to the other members of the family. The vertiginous coils of the snakes, the beaks of the vultures, the fangs of the rodents, the claws and talons of all the other beasts were right at their heels.

Doña Rosa came out of the house, followed by her three daughters, and when she saw the bizarre army she ordered the servants to attack it. . . . An entire battalion of slaves, a series of fires, and the overseer's hounds were all necessary to put that bestiary to flight. Even so, many of the strongest slaves and the biggest hounds were eaten alive.

To be precise, the Gamboa side lost in that battle: 99 pedigreed hounds, 17 breeding bitches, 1,208 fruit trees, 50 horses, and 326 slaves. The enemy side lost: 6,522 blind snakes, 7,000 mice, 9,001 rats, 33,333 vultures, 1 owl, 26 hawks, 75 wild dogs, 6 sparrowhawks, 1,250,020 bluetailed flies, 10,099 cockroaches, 908 slugs, 2 cranes, and 1 *almiquí* —the last of these tiny anteaters on the entire island.

Figures provided by Isabel Ilincheta.

Chapter XXVI

CONFUSION

At dusk, after dinner, the family and their guests (followed by the domestic slaves, who carried lanterns and armchairs) went out to the garden of the country house to enjoy the cool breezes and splendor of the insular evening. They were all excited about the preparations for the Christmas dinner they would enjoy the following night.

The slaves set up makeshift tables to serve the evening chocolate al fresco. Don Cándido Gamboa, after his third cup, tried to be cordial with his future daughter-in-law and engaged her in conversation.

"Isabel," he said, "I want you to take your place here as you would in your own home, and I hope you will enjoy yourself and have as much fun here as you would in your own charming estate in Alquízar."

No sooner had he said these kind words than doña Rosa, livid with fury, jumped to her feet, dashed a cup of hot chocolate in the face of a slave, and screamed:

"How dare you? How dare you flirt with Isabel right before my eyes and those of my daughters?"

"My dear," answered the impassive don Cándido, "no one's flirting with Isabel. I've simply been trying to make our future daughter-in-law feel at home."

"Hold it right there, don Cándido de Gamboa!" bellowed doña Rosa. "Leonardo has not chosen a wife, nor will he ever as long as I'm alive, because there's no woman—except me —who could love him, spoil him, put up with him, and understand him as he so richly deserves!"

"Rosa! Rosa!"

"Shut your mouth!" shouted doña Rosa, jabbing her elbow into her husband's ribs. "And don't say you haven't been flirting with Isabel! Don't you call that stuff about 'your own charming estate in Alquízar' flirting? To say nothing about having first said that you hoped she would 'enjoy herself' and 'have fun' in our own sacred home . . . ! Just what do you think you're doing, don Cándido de Gamboa?"

"Ma'am," Isabel amiably interrupted, "allow me to clear things up. My understanding of what don Cándido meant when he said, 'I hope you will have as much fun here as you would in your own charming estate in Alquízar,' was that he was talking about my house, not about me."

"And who knows for sure what his intention was?" replied doña Rosa, sticking to her guns.

"Well, only the author of the novel in which we're characters, Mr. Cirilo Villaverde, can know for sure," impartially responded Isabel.

"The author of the novel! The author of the novel! Don't give me that line, missy, because I've seen you do and say things the author of the novel you pretend to be a character in would never have allowed! Am I making myself clear?"

"Rosa! Rosa! Who gave you the right to offend Isabelita this way?" interjected don Cándido, truly pained.

"I have a perfect right," roared Rosa, "as a wife, a lady, and a mother! Either you bring me this 'Villa Verde' person to clear up this matter, or tomorrow I start divorce proceedings, beginning with a division of property which, of course, will ruin you! You heard me, don Cándido de Gamboa! I won't allow my daughters and me to be mocked!"

With that, doña Rosa burst into polonged sobs. All the young ladies and gentlemen, including, of course, the sugar-boy and Leonardo Gamboa, gathered around the lady, who was weeping copiously.

"God in heaven!" exclaimed don Cándido, raising his arms over his head. "How am I going to get Cirilo Villaverde to come here and clear up this misunderstanding (or bad reaction) when the degenerate swine escaped from the jail where he was serving a sentence for being a seditious criminal and fled north, where he lives plotting God knows what to ruin all of us?"

"Sir"—the elegant sugarboy approached don Cándido—"I can assure you that don Cirilo Villaverde is not up north but here, in Pinar del Río, not far from where we are standing."

"Are you sure?" asked the incredulous don Cándido. "How is it the police haven't nabbed him, then?"

"Because he's living in incognito. He's got a school up in

the hills, where he's teaching the peasant children and even the runaway slaves to read."

"Didn't I say he was a criminal, a delinquent?"

"Criminal or not," whimpered doña Rosa between sobs, "tomorrow we're going to see him so he can clear up this matter of 'your enchanting estate in Alquízar.' So let's all go to bed so we can be up first thing in the morning to hunt down this blessed gentleman. But don't think"—and here she turned her mortiferous gaze on don Cándido and Isabel—"you can pull the wool over my eyes that easily."

And, followed by a train of slaves and daughters, she went into the house.

Chapter XXVII

CIRILO VILLAVERDE

The sugarboy was absolutely right. Cirilo Villaverde, incognito, was bringing literacy to the rugged hills in the Sierra de los Organos in Pinar del Río.

It was easy to understand why he took up teaching: Having published his novel *Cecilia Valdés* in New York and already having published several other books in Cuba, he learned from his unquiet wife that not a single copy of any of them had ever been sold—after more than forty years! No one on the island—this was his only consolation—knew how to read.

Immediately, under orders form his willful wife, Villaverde, armed with notebooks and texts, left for Cuba. But because he had been sentenced to death by the colonial government he had to make a clandestine entrance into the mountains. Out in the bush, he built a school out of palm trees and branches.

When don Cándido, doña Rosa, their children, Isabel Ilincheta, and the sugarboy (their guide) reached the spot, Cirilo Villaverde was just getting ready to start classes. There were many students trudging (unwillingly, it must be said) up to that remote cabin. But not a single one of them—including an Indian, a race already extinct in Cuba—really wanted to learn to read. They all knew that the teacher's purpose was to have them read his novel, and rather than going through that torture they preferred to remain illiterate.

Besides, the classes weren't free, because Villaverde's wife kept an eye on him (and she was eagle-eyed) all the way from New York and wouldn't allow it. So each student had to pay for his lessons periodically, and because money didn't exist in that remote place, they paid in goods. One brought a chicken, another a suckling pig, this one a basket of eggs, that one some fresh eels. The most daring (the majority, that is) brought frogs, crabs, snakes, mice, and even spiders and scorpions, which the impassive Villaverde ordered placed in the covered barrels he had on one side of the classroom to store whatever came in. Orders from his implacable wife.

"Sir," a young mulatto was shouting, just when the visitors arrived, "my daddy sends you these turtles so you'll be quick and teach me the art of mathematics!"

"I don't teach mathematics, only reading!" answered Villaverde. And in a calmer voice: "In any case, put the turtles in the barrel over there and sit down."

"My mom sends you this sheep," shouted a barefoot girl. "It's payment for the whole semester."

"Tie it up and sit down," ordered the teacher as he prepared to call the roll.

It was then he noticed the visitors.

"May I help you?" he asked, standing up.

"Is it possible you don't recognize us?" complained don Cándido in a familiar tone.

"Of course I recognize you. But I never wrote that you were to come to see me, and much less here. I'm incognito and not 'in incognito' as you said a chapter ago, you fool!" he reproached the sugarboy.

"Well, here we are, 'Mister Incognito,'" ironically interjected doña Rosa. "And we're not leaving until you clear up an important matter for us, understand?"

"And just what is this 'important matter,' may I ask?" said Villaverde, clapping his spectacles onto his nose.

"Sir"—Isabel took the floor—"in the fourth chapter of the third part of your novel Cecilia Valdés you have don Cándido Gamboa say to Isabel Ilincheta, your humble servant, the following: 'Our house is your house. I hope you enjoy yourself and have as much fun here as you would in your own enchanting house in Alquízar.' What we want to know, as quickly as possible, is whether the part about 'your own enchanting house in Alquízar' alludes to me or just to the house."

"Oh well," said Villaverde, pausing as he gestured to the rioting students to keep still, "that's for the curious reader to decide...."

"None of that 'for the reader to decide' stuff!" protested the outraged doña Rosa. "You've got to decide this matter here and now—or I'm going to throw a fit!"

"Mama, please." Antonia tried to calm things down. "It may well be that he himself doesn't know what he meant."

"Well, if he doesn't know what he writes he ought to become a shoemaker or go haul cane down at the mill! He's going to clear this up now, and that's that!"

"Madam," said Villaverde, nervous and suffocating underneath his long beard and the European-style clothes his wife in New York had ordered him to wear despite the tropical climate, "I published the first volume of that novel in Lino Valdés's printing house in the middle of 1839...."

"So what?" bellowed doña Rosa. "Get to the point!"

"Then back in Havana in the year of 1842, without giving up my teaching post—"

"Shut up and start explaining!" interrupted don Cándido violently. "Because of you I'm on the point of losing my family...!"

Just then the sheep baaed and some of the students imitated them as they jumped for joy in their seats: Someone was finally putting that ridiculous schoolmaster in his place.

"Sock 'im!" one of them shouted.

"Pull 'is beard!" recommended another.

"Smack 'im ona head wit' da rula!" suggested a feminine voice.

"Over the better part of that epoch of patriotic delirium and dreams," Villaverde went on, really urgently in need of talking about his life and work, "the manuscript of the novel slept—"

"But, my dear sir, what the devil are you talking about?!" don Cándido shouted right into the author's face.

"Hard! Hard!" enthusiastically advised the Indian boy.

"So," Villaverde continued, "in no way can it be said that I spent forty years writing my novel."

"Enough is enough!" said doña Rosa at that moment.

And, picking up one of the barrels, she attempted to smash it over the teacher's head. But as she lifted it the lid fell off and what was inside poured out: a tangle of snakes. As if that weren't enough, doña Rosa picked up another barrel, which also opened, filling the place with enormous hairy spiders. But the indefatigable lady, despite the mortal danger she was in, could not contain herself. She picked up a third barrel and threw it on Villaverde's desk, where it smashed into a thousand pieces, releasing hundreds of land crabs all holding their

pincers on high. One of them seized the professor's rather
prominent nose in his gigantic claw and smashed his glasses.

Striking out blindly but without dropping the briefcase in
which he carried the day's lessons, Villaverde plunged right
through the palm-leaf wall of the cabin, which itself soon
collapsed. He went right on running, at an unheard-of speed
for a man his age dressed as he was, up and down the mountains.

"Catch the rat! Catch the rat!" his students, euphoric and
full of jubilation because their problems were over, shouted
after him. They quickly helped the ladies and gentlemen
escape from that place infested with dangerous animals.

On the way home, somewhat calmer, the visitors were
crossing one of the dangerous mountain passes and suddenly
heard a fearful shriek doubtlessly emitted by the old professor
still in the clutches of the stubborn crab.

"I wonder," doña Rosa said then, "if that idiot is finally
dead."

"Oh well," answered don Cándido, gallantly holding one
of his wife's pudgy hands, "that's for the curious reader to
decide."

Chapter XXVIII

CHRISTMAS DINNER

At nightfall on that twenty-fourth of December 1830, the Gamboa family and all their guests sat down to dinner. Christmas dinner was about to begin.

There were sixteen people, including, naturally, all the Gamboas, Isabel Ilincheta and her father, the priest, the doctor, the Yankee technician, the majordomo, the mayor of Mariel, the sugarboy, and a few other local figures.

Behind each person at table, there were two slaves struggling to keep the diner's plate full, while the overseer, wielding a silent whip (the gentlefolk wanted no extraneous noise at the table), made sure the rest of the servants brought the innumerable dishes at the appropriate moment. Under the table another set of guests was toiling away: the dogs, cats, chickens, and domestic pigs the family allowed on that sacred day to enjoy the bones and other leftovers the diners would throw to them as proof of their Christian charity.

The dinner began when two gigantic platters appeared, one overflowing with eels swimming in oil and rice in the Valencian style and the other piled high with stuffed turkeys and partridges. These were accompanied by a caldron filled with black Christmas beans. Hot on the heels of these came a fried cow and a crate containing eight hundred sweet potatoes. Every bit of it, what doña Rosa termed "the appetizer," was rapidly gobbled up by the enthusiastic company, who paused only long enough to remove from their laps the feet and snouts of the animals grunting or barking in anticipation of their rations.

Doña Rosa clapped her hands, and the second course was served.

Sixteen crispy suckling pigs, sixteen gigantic clay pots filled with crabs in hot sauce, sixteen pans of cod in tomato sauce, sixteen racks of goat, a huge pot of chili sauce mixed with stewed *jutía,* a roast Santa María python, corn bread, cassava bread, roast *malanga* and plantains.

"And where the devil are the tripes?" shouted doña Rosa in exaltation.

Instantly six powerful slaves respectfully deposited a kind of tub on the table, filled with tripes and stewed okra Creole style.

"Fish!" bellowed doña Rosa.

Fifty slaves brought in a manatee caught in Mariel Bay and steamed in sour sauce, pan sugar, and monkey oil.

"The sausages!" ordered the hostess once again.

And immediately in burst the master chef himself carrying, to ingratiate himself with his mistress, an enormous platter where myriad sausages coiled, swimming in pork fat and fried eggs.

"The hare!"

At which each diner squared off and dispatched five of those delicious animals.

"Drinks!" ordered don Cándido.

And next to each lady appeared a tub of custard apple punch, another filled with cane juice and pepper punch, another filled with anise liqueur, another filled with absinthe, and half a dozen filled with red wine. As for the gentlemen: Each one drank a barrel of La Viuda champagne, another of French cognac, and another of Desnoes rum, manufactured by that merchant in Jamaica.

"I'm just getting in the mood to eat," the doctor said at that moment.

Without hesitating, doña Rosa ordered the chef to bring in the special dishes she'd personally ordered him to prepare with all the skill his prodigious talent could muster.

In a flash the table was covered by platters of iguana in green sauce, octopus in coconut milk, hummingbird livers, oysters in orchid sauce, turtles in Chinese sauce, ornithorhynchus eggs, fritters in caviar, crocodile cracklings, magpie tongues, reindeer meatballs, water buffalo hearts stuffed with stingray roe, and seal fetuses—these latter derived from pregnant seals brought by ship from Cape Hatteras and forced to miscarry a few hours before dinner. Just to list a few of the delicacies.

"The cheese!" demanded doña Rosa, shouting over the chaos.

"Dessert!" shouted don Cándido in an ecstasy of delight and euphoria.

"Coffee!" exclaimed the Gamboa girls.

"Chocolate!" hastily added don Pedro, another lover of that drink.

"Punch!" demanded the doctor.

"Hot cane juice!" the sugarboy insisted.

"What about the salad?" remembered the Yankee technician.

"They've forgotten the Christmas nougat," pointed out the priest, who found it easy to blend his religion and his appetite.

Instantly the whole table was covered with a complicated selection of cheeses, candies, drinks, salads, celebrated dishes, nougats, and huge cups of steaming chocolate.... Stewed *bejuco* got mixed with French champagne, meringues from Morón collided with nougats from Jijón, papaya was eaten wrapped in Westphalian ham, guavas in syrup were eaten with fritters, and sturgeon swam in rice pudding.... Double candied egg yolk sweetmeats made by Florencio García Cisneros himself rained on the table, along with corn bread, cassava, chimpanzee brains swimming in cane juice, candied sea turtle eggs, ducks in sweet sauce, honeycombs, spiced cornmeal wrapped in plantain leaves, quinces, sugarcane, shrimps in molasses, cream cakes, Provençal cheeses, dried figs, frog legs, parsley, deer testicles, heads of sea horses.... Main courses and appetizers, desserts and roasts, appeared and just as quickly were devoured in an incessant whirlwind that instead of satisfying the hunger of the guests only whipped it higher.

By midnight, when dinner was over, everyone had turned into gigantic, shining balls, bodies that were completely spherical which the servants covered with enormous shawls and carefully pushed into their respective rooms. But despite the care exercised by these household slaves, some of those huge human spheres went astray and rolled out of the house. They crossed—destroying it instantly—the garden and scattered over the countryside, followed by the faithful retainers who tried in vain to catch up with them.

It was truly poetic to see those colossal spheres shining in the moonlight sliding swiftly over the fields which were already wet with dew. Behind them ran diminutive, dark figures with poles, ropes, and even cattle prods, trying to stop them.

For a long time, the plantation slaves, who were trying to keep warm outside their straw huts by sitting around small fires, could observe those balls vertiginously spinning around the countryside. Then they crashed into the Sierra de los Organos, a chain of mountains that strongly resembled the great organs found in cathedrals. And those organs began to play, doubtlessly enchanted by such large and unforeseen visitors.

Those transformed into rolling spheres were the priest, doña Rosa and her daughters Antonia and Adela, don Pedro, the majordomo, the doctor, and the sugarboy—who may well have rolled out on his own account, chasing after the woman he loved.

Naturally, smashing against the mountains changed the course of those voluminous travelers and careened them into the Viñales Valley, where gravity stopped them forever, transforming them into the geological accident known today as the Viñales Boulders. . . . The sugarboy's fate was somewhat different because his love for Adela kept him alive just a bit longer. He made a violent attempt to reach the boulder which had once been his beloved, hit her, and rebounded toward Oriente Province, where he died, alone, on the coast of Matanzas. Today he is the formidable elevation known around the world as the Matanzas Sugar Loaf.

The following day, don Cándido left the plantation in a comfortable coach, accompanied by Carmen and Leonardo, the only two members of his family to survive. As they passed through the Viñales Valley he recognized the now-petrified figure of his wife and, fearing she might still reproach him for something, ordered his driver to speed up.

Part Five

THE RETURN

Chapter XXIX

THE MIRACLE

So, Leonardo Gamboa had tricked her and had gone out to the country with that peasant, thought the outraged Cecilia Valdés as she paced, or rather ran, around the small room knocking down doña Josefa, who was observing her. "So the miserable rat forgot me after all his promises, after he swore he would marry me! And here I am, left on the shelf! A fool! And pregnant into the bargain . . . with a child I don't want to have. Because I want nothing more to do with its father! I want nothing from him! I'll never, ever love him again! Ever! I hope I never see him again! And as for this son of his—at least I hope it'll be a son and not a daughter—I'll do everything I can to keep it from being born. To give birth to a fatherless mulatto in this world is to bring another slave into the world. No, I don't want that crime on my conscience!"

Cecilia ended up shouting at the top of her lungs as she squeezed and punched her stomach, where the unborn child was growing.

"Ah, I see, so you don't love me, eh?" said the small fetus from within Cecilia's womb. "Well, now you'll see."

And in under five minutes, gathering an unprecedented amount of energy, the fetus grew at a monstrous pace within the placenta until it reached the size it would have been at term. As it changed position it kicked its mother in the stomach just to annoy her. And then it began to butt its way out, screaming all the way. As the baby girl—another blow to Cecilia—emerged from her body, Cecilia remained in a state of shock.

"Mama," the little girl said in a flash, two years old in two seconds. Her rapid growth stopped at that point.

Even more alarmed now, Cecilia contemplated that diminutive mulatta who held out her arms to her and who was herself in miniature—although perhaps a bit darker.

"Damn him! Damn him!" exclaimed Cecilia, always thinking about her unfaithful lover. "Look what you've done to me. I'll never forgive you. I'll never forgive this shameful crime, even if you were to beg me down on your knees. A skunk, just like all the rest!"

Just then Leonardo came in through the front door. He had just returned from La Tinaja and immediately ran out to see Cecilia because he knew how much it mortified don Cándido, who absolutely forbade Leonardo to see her.

"Are you alone?" he asked her.

"Yes, yes!" Cecilia answered, forgetting in the twinkling of an eye her hatred for Leonardo as well as the existence of her grandmother and daughter.

"Were you waiting for me?"

"With all my heart and soul."

"Who told you I'd be back today?"

"My heart."

"You're paler and thinner."

"I've suffered so much thinking about you. . . . Leonardo, promise me we'll get married: We have a daughter now."

"Soon, soon we'll get married," promised the young lawyer, who was thinking about announcing his engagement and prompt marriage to Isabel Ilincheta that night at the Philharmonic Society ball. He naturally never gave a second thought to the fact that he had sired a daughter with this mulatta.

Besides, was Cecilia mad? Where had she found that pickaninny who was shouting "Daddy" at him and reaching out her arms to him? What kind of crude tricks was this mulatta up to, trying to tangle him up like that? These black bitches are real devils, he thought. He said:

"Wouldn't it be better to talk this over alone in the kitchen?"

And in they went, closing the curtain behind them.

Still paralyzed in a corner of the room, doña Josefa had seen everything. Once again the same curse that had fallen on the family had taken its toll. The handsome, fleeting, and inevitable white man had sired yet another mulatta so the vicious cycle might begin anew.

The story had begun with her mother, doña Amalia, a black from Africa, who had given birth to her, Josefa, an almost-black mulatta, and she, with another white man, had given birth to the lighter Rosario Alarcón, who in turn, with don Cándido Gamboa, had given birth to Cecilia, an almost-white (or high yellow as they say), and now Cecilia, with her own white brother, had given birth to a daughter who, doubly condemned, would doubtless fall in love with some white.

The great-grandmother had noticed how the child stared in fascination, not daughterly affection, at Leonardo. Doña Josefa was giving up. No pain, she thought, is as great as mine. And from the kitchen came, as a confirmation of her suspicions, the laughter of Cecilia and Leonardo. As if that weren't enough, her great-granddaughter pulled on her hem to remind her she too was there. Really, she could stand no more, doña Josefa said to herself, and she ran to the room where the painful image of the Virgin pierced by the fiery sword stood. Only she could offer some consolation, work some miracle.

She went down on her knees before the Virgin and Child, weeping her eyes out and asking how it was possible that life be such an absolute hell, how it could be that there could exist another hell in the next world, and, above all, why should she try to avoid that other hell if she could never forget these sufferings. . . . How was it possible that her pain was only increased with more and more grief? "How is it possible"—she was shouting now—"that no one even comes to ask why I'm weeping, why I've been weeping all my life, why I'm still alive? . . . How is it possible that not even you"—and she raised her eyes to the statue—"make me a sign of encouragement, work no miracles for me? Can it be that you don't understand that even though I have my heart wrapped in steel and nailed shut with copper I can't stand any more?"

Then the Virgin pierced by the sword of fire shuddered slightly in her niche and, yielding up a cold and fearsome stare to the mulatta, said:

"And how is it possible that you've chosen me of all people to be your consolation? With this fiery sword piercing my breast year in and year out, with my only son murdered by the mob, how can I be the one in charge of comforting you? Haven't you realized (no one ever realizes it!) that I too am worn out with pain? How is it possible that seeing me like this, over so many centuries, no one has understood that I the symbol of despair and not happiness? . . . I'm the one"—and here her voice, doubly virginal because it was the first time she'd ever spoken, became more powerful—"and no you (none of you) who bears the supreme suffering! I'm no salvation, and if all of you have taken me for what I'm not, whose fault is it? Did I ever talk about salvation? Forget that stuff." Now she was imperturbably giving orders. "And take pity on me. I on my own simply cannot stand or even describe my pain anymore. I cannot go on for all eternity in this position, with this fiery sword sticking out of me. Have some consideration. Sacrifice yourself! *You* work a miracle.... Help *me!*"

After she heard these words, doña Josefa's long-suffering heart gave out, and despite the fact, as she herself said, that incessant grief had bound her heart in steel and nailed it shut with copper, an absolute, irremediable anguish overwhelmed her and burst in her bosom.... Then one of those copper nails holding her heart together broke and flew toward the statue of the Virgin and knocked it to the floor, where it burst into a thousand pieces.

When Cecilia and Leonardo decided to finish off their loving reunion in the bedroom, they stopped for an instant when they discovered pieces of marble on the floor. Pieces of marble anyone would have thought belonged to the statue of the Virgin pierced by the fiery sword, if it weren't for the fact that the statue was still standing on its pedestal.

But if the lovers had looked carefully, which of course they did not, they would have noticed that the Virgin had been transformed. Her skin had darkened, her hair had become kinky, the child in her arms was not blond but a little pickaninny, and her face wore an even greater expression of grief. An expression that increased when the brother and sister fell onto the bed in each other's arms.

"Look! Look!" shouted Cecilia and Leonardo's daughter, jumping up and down next to the bed. "Grandma's turned into stone!"

But they were in no mood to listen to such silly talk.

Chapter XXX

ON LOVE

A great love is satisfied desire, unleashed violence. It is adventure and fleetingness both enjoyed to the full precisely because they are ephemeral. Because if a great love were something eternal and unavoidable, it would be a burden, a punishment, and, above all (and this is the worst), a bore....These were Leonardo Gamboa's thoughts as he ran toward Cecilia. A plenitude and an overflowing, that's what love is. "Passion, if excessive, cannot be beautiful." That's Pascal himself I'm quoting. Yes, Blaise Pascal, whose wisdom I learned directly from Professor Javier de la Cruz in the College of San Carlos. I'm an educated man, I'll have you understand, even if the imbecile who's writing this novel depicts me as an idle, lazy fool and a bad student....I know about Pascal and a lot of other things. Above all, I really know what love is because I'm alive and young and healthy and strong. There is absolutely no connection between me and the escapades that syphilitic degenerate who thinks he's Goya himself (I mean Arenas, of course) ascribes to me or those other pranks the other old idiot, who also was just as incapable of accurately depicting my character or anything else....Love, I'll continue now, is either explosion or death. "When we don't love in excess, we don't love enough." (Now I've finished with Pascal.) Because a man's heart is like one of those horrible cities in the north: Either you melt in the heat or die of the cold. And naturally all that takes place, like the climate in those hideous cities, in stages. Right now I'm in the fire stage, and that's how I hope to be forever, or at least for a long, long time. I'm not going to throw away the opportunity I've got in front of me and I'm not going to tie myself down if I don't want to.

To love is to materialize in a flash the miracle of being alive. What meaning can life have beyond the most voluptuous desires totally satisfied right where they appear to us, in the object that provokes them? That object for me now is Celia or Cecilia (those two idiot authors use both names), that stupendous mulatta who reminds me for some reason or other of my sister Adela.

Everyone, even Cecilia, is always telling me about commitment, about rules, about obligations—even when they talk about love. No sir! Love cannot be bound by any kind of commitment or tie; no law (except its own) can mediate it because then it wouldn't be love. It would be obligation, responsibility, a bother. That's why there are wives, families, friends. Love is this: bursting into your lover's house at dawn, carrying her off to bed, and possessing her right then and there, before desire can be abated by talk, questions, reproaches, or complaints. A great love has to be a conquest, a prohibited and punishable act, a mockery of all that surrounds us, that orders and oppresses us, and above all a feeling of being absolutely free and independent of the loved object.

A great love asks no questions, presupposes no future: Because it is great it can only exist in the present, and because if we were to think "This is a great love," we would treat it as such and it would automatically cease to be a great love. Free, no strings attached, even frivolous—these are some of the requirements that have to be met if you want to enjoy a great love. . . . Play, unkept promises, infidelity, pride challenged and trampled, then raised up, kissed, adored, and immediately abandoned, then returned to, always with the certainty that this will be the last time. This is something else that has to be observed if you want a great love. . . . Because in order for a great love to exist you can't have just one lover. That would be too little for us and too much for her. She would end up boring us and (which is much the same thing) betraying us. You have to have various, numerous, many lovers if you really want to love and you love only one, to whom you give with true vitality and abundance the specific, unique fruit of your lasting love.

Another absolutely necessary requirement for the proper development of passion is someone who opposes our relationships. Because a great love is above all a great caprice; because a great love is above all the egoism of two bodies that reflect each other and desire each other reciprocally. Because a great love, in order to be one, should never—as I said earlier—believe it is one, and should never, ever think about what love is, because if love had an explanation it wouldn't be love but a book, a fable, or some other story for pious old ladies or desperate young ladies. . . . Revealed passion, discharged anxiety, violated virtue, showing that one is alive and triumphant, vanity, possession, ecstasy, and culmination—both spiritual and physical—in the face of the other's subjected, angry vanity, joyfully subjected, passing from proud lover to nervous, fearful, insecure beloved.

A great love means two burning, anxious bodies that find each other by means of desire and that in possessing each other become all loved and hated bodies—sister and mother, father and friends. Everything that in some way confirms our being alive and our most seditious, invincible feelings.

Because a great love is, above all, a great provocation.

Chapter XXXI

THE PHILHARMONIC SOCIETY BALL

That thirty-first of December, the grand annual ball at the Philharmonic Society had a double meaning and a double importance. The first: The assassination of the English consul and admiral lord Clarence Paget—an assassination planned by the captain general himself with the complicity of don Cándido de Gamboa as well as other plantation owners and slave dealers—was to occur there. The second: The wedding of Leonardo Gamboa and Isabel Ilincheta was to be announced there to the select company.

At nightfall the guests began to arrive, wearing enormous masks that completely blinded them, and, as if the masks weren't enough, they also wore blindfolds under their masks. Feeling their way along, they crossed the enormous hall and, as soon as they were against the wall on which the colossal portrait of king Fernando VII of Spain was hung, they removed the uncomfortable but lifesaving blindfolds. Of course, it must be observed that many ladies transformed that act of self-preservation into an exquisite display of coquetry by wearing fabulous pitch-black veils studded over with precious stones and embroidered in gold.

Why was it that the crème de la crème of the Havana nobility entered that noble salon blindfolded? The colossal portrait of Fernando VII nailed to the huge rear wall dominated the entire space, and its features were so horrifying (which is to say, they reproduced the king's features so well) that everyone who had seen it to date had died instantly. It wasn't simply a matter of an outsized, diabolical mouth, huge, pointed ears, a gigantic triple chin, sparse, ashen hair, a spectral, depraved face, a harrowing nose, or bulging, sinister eyes—all of which that fearsome face did possess. It was the overall effect

—such an awe-inspiring charge of horror and malignity, of bestiality and stupidity, all within the limits of a single face, that no living creature could face it.

No doubt some curious and impertinent reader (these are never lacking) might wish to interrupt me at this precise moment—this tense and difficult moment in my story—to ask me how I could possibly give such a faithful and detailed description of the portrait. Very simple, my dear sir: I am the artist, its creator—Francisco de Goya y Lucientes, at your service. . . . I did a perfect piece of work there, and the canvas contains all my fury, all my genius, and all my syphilitic lucidity (an honor conferred on me directly, with no masks, by queen María Luisa). When the portrait was finished, Fernando VII ordered it covered with a double canvas, not to protect it but to protect himself.

That portrait of mine has taken part successfully in many military campaigns, in the most famous conflicts. It caused the extermination of all the Indians in the Antilles and in a large part of what is the southern United States today. It created the immense deserts that exist today in the various continents. Then, because His Majesty's hatred for Cuba was so great, above all because certain noble criollos requested some reforms, he ordered the portrait (or fearsome weapon) to be hung in the center of the most elegant Havana salon. But the Cubans, in general a roguish and shameless but astute lot, discovered the royal trick and attempted to get around it. They were not allowed to cover the portrait. Nor could they take it down. Would they simply not attend balls held at the Philharmonic Society? They'd rather die. The solution: Don't look at the portrait. That's why they all entered the magnificent hall with their eyes blindfolded until they could stand with the painting at their backs. The orchestra, two hundred blind blacks (extremely prudent men: They took the precaution of blinding themselves), played with their backs to the painting.

The elegant ladies, floating like balloons inside their hoopskirts, were now dancing a contradanse with their backs to the painting. Many of them carried monkeys dressed up in French costume, clearly imitating the countess of Merlín who imposed that custom on the beautiful habaneras, who thought they were echoing the dernier cri of Paris. Also standing with their backs to the wall and right under the huge portrait were the bishop of Havana, the nefarious Echerre, the commandant f the Spanish flotilla, the mayor of Havana, the procurator, on Cándido Gamboa with his daughter Carmen, and Tondá, wearing his saber and gold epaulets. All were grouped around he captain general, Dionisio Vives, solemn in his official ash, ruff, sword, gold command staff, with his tricorne under is arm.

"Here they come! Here they come!" Don Cándido hissed ut the announcement as soon as he saw the impeccable fig-res of the English consul and lord Clarence Paget enter the all, led in by the peerless Maria de la O, an almost-white ulatta who that night, under the express orders of the captain eneral, served as hostess for the prominent dignitaries.

The huge orchestra stopped playing. Ladies and gentlemen emained standing in anticipation of the fatal and breathlessly esired finale. But the two guests advanced looking down ntil they were before the captain general, and, with the most xquisite, courtly style, they bowed to the maximum public gure and the bishop, paying their profoundest respects.

"Make yourselves at home," said the captain general as he ade a sweeping gesture and asked, "What do you think of e hall?"

"Very beautiful," said the consul, still staring at the gold uckles on his shoes.

"Quite . . ." said lord Clarence Paget, his gazed fixed on he floor, and remaining silent thereafter, his stock of Spanish uite exhausted.

"Take a good look at everything," Dionisio Vives virtually rdered. "This building is the pride of the kingdom. And as ar as the paintings are concerned . . ." And here the captain eneral pointed behind him as he thought, *Some bastard's etrayed us! Son of a bitch! Tomorrow I arrest the whole amn city!* "The paintings are really extraordinary, created by e best painter in the royal court."

"Masterpieces," agreed the consul with his eyes tightly hut.

"The gentle María de la O will take charge of showing you e hall," finished the captain general. He gestured, and the rchestra, in homage to the visitors, played a slow minuet and en an allemande.

By midnight, the guests had consumed tons of food and finite barrels of wine, emptying again and again the long bles where refreshments were served. They left the hall

rarely—to go out to the central patio to walk to the recently
excavated well, where they vomited. This new and lifesaving
custom was adopted by the habaneros as a direct result of the
tragic events that took place after the Christmas dinner held
out at the La Tinaja plantation. This is why all the mansions
in Havana (and even those in the country) now have beautiful
wells in the very center of their patios.

Don Cándido was so preoccupied with the collapse of the
plans that he even forgot to order Leonardo to announce his
forthcoming marriage. Nor did the distinguished gentleman
notice the looks the black Tondá was casting at his daughter
Carmen, looks that the Gamboa heiress received with true
delight. Not even when Tondá put his arm around the young
lady's waist and danced a waltz and two Spanish dances with
her did don Cándido emerge from his trance.

It was after four in the morning, and the English guests had
still not looked at the portrait of Fernando VII.

"A pair of pigs. They've ruined the party," murmured the
captain general, always smiling and bowing.

"Quite . . ." answered lord Clarence Paget, who of course
understood not a word, with a bow.

But it was in that instant, nevertheless, when an unforeseen
event almost brought the plans of Havana high life to fruition.

As the consul was dancing with the statuesque Maria de la
O, he accidentally and disastrously stepped on the twitching
tail of the nervous monkey the lady held on a fine and long
golden chain. The poor little animal, reacting to the weight of
that powerful boot, escaped from the mulatta and fearfully
scampered up the rear wall until it was even with the colossal
portrait. But when its tiny eyes met the canvas, the monkey
gave out the loudest shriek that ever reverberated in that hall.

It was impossible for almost all those present not to turn to
look at the place from which those screams had come. Then,
in less time than it takes lightning to flash across the sky, the
immense salon was filled with cadavers. Almost every
member of Havana high society died at that party.

Among the survivors were, in addition to the two hundred
black musicians, the captain general (whose iron ruff, secretly
fashioned for this event, kept him from turning his head), don
Cándido de Gamboa, who copied all the gestures of the captain general and therefore did not move, as well as Isabel
Ilincheta and Leonardo Gamboa, who stood gazing into

space, calculating the combined value of their two fortunes. Of course, His Excellency the English consul general and admiral lord Clarence Paget also survived. "A strange party these Indians have given," commented the consul as he picked his way through (and sometimes over) dead bodies, leaving the sepulchral hall in great dignity.

"Quite . . ." added lord Clarence Paget, cautiously following the consul.

With regard to Carmen and Tondá: Oblivious to anything except their own passion, they took advantage of the catastrophe to commandeer the bishop's carriage (his illustrious person wouldn't be needing it ever again) and rush full speed through the city wall into the open country, where Carmen lost her virginity in a split second.

Chapter XXXII

THE WEDDING

The deaths of doña Rosa, Adela, and even don Pedro, facilitated don Cándido's plan to marry Leonardo to Isabel Ilincheta. He knew that Isabel's father loved her too much to give her to any living man and that the same applied to Leonardo's mother and younger sister: Their love for Leonardo was so intense that for one reason or another they could never find a woman worthy of the young man—except, perhaps, themselves. . . . There was only one obstacle: Cecilia Valdés.

But don Cándido, in order to make Leonardo forget his lover, had offered him (knowing full well how ambitious Leonardo was) both his entire fortune (a kind of dowry) and the brand-new title of Count of the House of Gamboa. He had paid yet another fortune to the monarchs of Spain for the title, which was due to arrive at any moment, a moment don Cándido had been longing for with the greatest anticipation, the moment when all his labors would be rewarded. Besides, according to don Cándido and his wise lawyers, the fortune and the title would remain within the house of Gamboa because the husband—by law—was charged with administering them. In any case, with Isabel in the family the fortune would not only be safe but would probably multiply at a prodigious rate.

The preparations were rapidly made, and on the sixth of January, the feast of the Three Kings, while all the poor folk were celebrating and having a good time with masks and dancing at the foot of and on top of the city wall, the ladies who had survived the disaster of the Philharmonic Society (because they hadn't gone) marched, wearing black and draped with mantillas, to the lofty Church of the Angel.

Naturally the usual busybodies informed Cecilia Valdés of the impending marriage of her lover to Isabel Ilincheta. Nemesia Pimienta herself, growing more and more resentful by the day, spiteful and jealous, but still clinging to the remote hope of one day being Leonardo Gamboa's lover, personally informed Cecilia. Enraged, wild with fury, and brandishing a huge kitchen knife, Cecilia Valdés dashed out of the house and ran from one end of the city to the other. Finally, in despair, she lurched into the tailor shop where José Dolores Pimienta was working.

"José Dolores! José Dolores!" Cecilia bellowed, for the first time in her life embracing the mulatto who idolized her. "This marriage must not take place."

"Well then, Celia my love, it will not take place," said the young man as he took the knife and walked out into the street.

Then, her hair in a tangle, her dress akimbo, Cecilia shouted to him once more:

"José Dolores, don't hurt him! Get her! Only her!"

So few words never before caused so much pain to a human being. At that moment José Dolores Pimienta understood just how much Cecilia loved Leonardo and how much she despised him. But the mulatto restrained himself from shouting at Cecilia the word that was about to spring from his lips and ran toward the church.

At the base of the immense stairway that leads up to the cathedral, don Cándido Gamboa, impeccably dressed, hat in hand, stood greeting one and all. Numerous ladies who had left their carriages below joined the already large throng inside. The church was packed, and the altar shone, magnificently decorated with all kinds of flowers and thousands of candles.

A select chorus of altar boys from the college of the Belenite fathers entoned a "Salve." Then the wedding music began as Isabel Ilincheta made her way down the long nave, dressed in a long, brilliant dress of white silk, a veil worked with gold, and carrying a gigantic branch of orange blossoms. Next to her, wearing a morning coat, marched Leonardo.

The bride and groom had just reached the last step to the altar, where the priest and the other officiants were waiting to bring the ceremony to its climax, when a mulatto, his hat pulled down over his eyes, suddenly darted out from among the columns, collided with Leonardo, and instantly disappeared on the opposite side.

Leonardo raised his hand to his breast and softly moaned as he leaned on Isabel's arm. The knife had entered his left breast and penetrated straight to his heart.

Isabel, the only person to witness the murder, instantly understood that if the marriage were not to take place, the Gamboa fortune would not pass into her hands. So, flashing a radiant smile to the entire assembly, she jammed the end of her branch of orange blossoms into her fiancé's wound to stanch the flow of blood while with her other powerful arm she dragged Leonardo to the altar, where the priest noted with alarm how the bridegroom grew paler and paler. The bride answered all the ceremonial questions, lowering her voice to answer for Leonardo. Rapidly and dexterously she herself effected the exchange of wedding bands, and, always smiling, she kissed his cheeks as she held him up. . . . But, astute beyond her years, she understood right then and there that if she had no child by that dying man, don Cándido's lawyers, "those wise and sinister vermin" (she said to herself), would have her disinherited.

So, to the astonishment of priests, nuns, altar boys, and the entire distinguished company, Isabel Ilincheta, right at the altar, had herself penetrated by the dying young man, taking full (as she knew herself) advantage of the final spasm that all dying men experience.

An indignant and loud roar of protest and shock echoed throughout the church.

Now that the legal forms had been observed, the widow pulled the branch of orange blossoms out of the wound. The stanched blood, under even greater pressure because of the sexual strain, gushed forth in a powerful jet, soaking the bride's regal gown as well as the faces of the first few rows of guests.

Another indignant and loud roar of protest and shock echoed throughout the church.

"After the murderer! After him! Catch the man who murdered my husband!" shouted Isabel, pointing toward the columns where José Dolores Pimienta had disappeared much earlier.

A third indignant and loud roar of protest echoed throughout the church. And almost all those present ran out in pursuit of José Dolores Pimienta, who by then, having taken advantage of the day's festivities, had scampered over the city wall and was already deep in the virgin lands beyond.

Don Cándido, bearing the weight of complete defeat, returned to his home later that afternoon. In a flash, the entire fortune of the Gamboa family had passed into Isabel Ilincheta's hands. And, as if that weren't enough, his only son had been murdered by a mulatto and his beloved daughter Carmen had run away with a black. He was now the laughingstock of the entire city and had caused such an uproar that the captain general (unconsolable at the loss of his protégé) accused him of corrupting the young black and ordered him to leave the country. He would have to go in the very condition he had come, but now he was an old man.

But to suffer dishonor at the hands of a black and to suffer economic ruin at the same time were things don Cándido Gamboa could not bear.

"Tirso!" he ordered. "Bring the three-legged brazier."

The slave appeared on the double with the gigantic and smoking brazier and stopped before his master. He was disconcerted to see that don Cándido had no cigar prepared for lighting.

Don Cándido slowly raised his eyes and saw the half-dressed and barefoot black holding the enormous silver artifact on high.

"Hit me over the head with that brazier!"

The slave gently tapped his master's head.

"Listen, boy," said don Cándido, his voice low but full of fury, "split my head in two with that brazier or I'll kill you."

When he heard that bizarre order, the black did not hesitate. He raised the three-legged brazier as high as he could and with all the held-in rage of a lifetime brought it down with such force on don Cándido's head that he broke it, not in two but into hundreds of pieces, spattering the walls and furniture of the beautiful mansion.

Having witnessed that spectacle, and fearing the imminent gendarmes, along with the terrifying agents of Cantalapiedra or Tondá himself who would certainly hang them on the spot, the slaves ran for their lives. But not before looting the house from top to bottom.

The next day, the postman banged the bronze knocker on the front door several times. When no one answered, he tossed a long parchment document into the house through the entry patio. It was the title of Count of the House of Gamboa, which the Spanish monarch had finally deigned to send to don Cándido. An old black woman who had been left behind unrolled the scroll but, seeing nothing of value in it, was about to throw it away. Just then it began to rain, so she used the parchment as an umbrella and silently slipped out of the house. By the time she'd reached Monserate Gate, heading toward the Lagunas and Pocitos districts, the letters and the royal seal on the title were completely washed away.

CONCLUSION

At the insistence of Isabel Ilincheta, Cecilia Valdés was condemned, as an accessory to the murder of Leonardo Gamboa, to one year in jail. She was sent to the Convent or House of the Penitents of Paula, where she found her mother, Rosario Alarcón. Rosario recognized her daughter and recovered her sanity simultaneously. When Cecilia had finished serving her sentence, Rosario was waiting for her at the prison gates, and there she told Cecilia who she really was. That is, that Leonardo Gamboa was her brother.

"No wonder we loved each other so much," sighed Cecilia as she embraced her mother.

As for Carmen and Tondá: Chased by the troops of the captain general himself, who never forgave his favorite for betraying him, they found refuge in a settlement of runaway slaves. As soon as they arrived, they met Dionysius, who had been brought there by Dolores Santa Cruz, who had also nursed him back to health. Dionysius became the communal cook, turning out really exquisite stews. For her part, Dolores Santa Cruz regularly showed off, to the delight of the children of Carmen and Tondá (disgusting little mulatto brats), the countess's beautiful hair.

Years went by, and Dolores Santa Cruz, still disguised as a mad beggar, learned on one of her forays into Havana that José Dolores Pimienta had still not been captured. She also learned that Cecilia Valdés's daughter was already a tall and *ex-crazy* (her emphasis) girl who day and night wandered the plazas and streets and talked in secret with Leonardo Junior—infuriating the mother of the handsome lad, the countess doña Isabel de Ilincheta y Gamboa. "As regards Cecilia," added Dolores sadly, putting on and taking off the wig, "she's just not the same. She's put on too much weight, goes to church a lot, and only comes to her window to call her daughter home. Of course, her daughter never even answers her."

117

Chapter XXXIII

ON LOVE

Blood in the temple. Sacrifice and scandal. That's how it was, that's how a great love had to be. Because a great love Cecilia now thinks to herself as she makes her way, with difficulty, up Angel Hill, cannot submit to the norms and conventions and laws that would slowly strangle it, turning it into just one more routine in our daily death. A great love had to be violent, unique, and brief, an explosion that incinerates us—body and soul. It reduces the rest of our lives to ash through which we plod, making our solitary way, stimulated now only by our memories.

Jealousy, desire, suffering, loneliness that time turns into a tranquil pleasure, a fleeting delight that becomes glorious because it is lost and brief. Seeing ourselves there, far away and unrepeatable, one last time each inside the other, and to enjoy now, precisely now, more than ever that moment which, if it had prolonged itself, would have become a bore.... A love, a great love, what was it if not the illusion that we nurture, we mystify, we feed with our very solitude, with our very misery and with our very love? Thus had she glorified and mystified what in Leonardo was nothing more than a passing desire, a vanity, even satisfied vulgarities. How she, all of us in fact, had turned (and go on turning) the lover's coarsest gesture into the sublimest actions! And in the face of those actions we give in, just as we give in to those actions. And in time those actions that never were extraordinary or noble or sublime but simply manifestations of vitality, futile caprices fleeting excesses rapidly satisfied and forgotten, acquire almost magic, sacred, inconceivable dimensions.... Now she understood it, now she understood it all, and she regretted nothing.

Because a great love is not even the story of a great deception or a cruel betrayal that takes us by surprise and leaves us only the void of our perplexity. No, a great love is the simple story of a self-deception that we impose on ourselves, that we suffer, and that we enjoy. Gestures we know to be circumstantial that we magnify; promises that are forgotten with the same force they are spoken; we treasure things sworn we know will never be done; and we exalt all these things thanks to which and for which we live. Because a great love is not the story of a great love but its invention.

That this invention is impossible, that it ends in mockery, or that it is cut off just when we were exalting it are the basic requirements for it to enter the category of great love. Now she understood it all. And she understood more: She clearly understood that her marriage ceremony had taken place years before in the church on Angel Hill. Because it was in that moment, when Leonardo, arm in arm with Isabel Ilincheta, was stabbed and murdered, when the absolute and truly sacred union between Cecilia and Leonardo took place. Because a great love is also the story of a failure or an irreparable loss.

These were Cecilia's thoughts as she once again entered the Church of the Angel, the only place she visited frequently these days. People thought she went there to beg forgiveness, but the fact is that she ascended Angel Hill only to give thanks to heaven for having granted her the grace of knowing what a great love is. A knowledge which, if Leonardo's death (or sacrifice) had not taken place in the flower of his youth, she never would have had.

Thus—as she fell to her knees—she was truly thankful to the gods.

Chapter XXXIV

ON LOVE

Was she cold? Was she hungry? Could she be in some danger? Would someone take advantage of her helpless condition? Would someone try to rape her? Was someone raping her at that very moment? Or has she given herself to someone out of misery or simply out of pure pleasure while I, hidden and hunted, wander and call her name? Could she be alone, as alone as I am? Would she remember me from time to time, would she think fondly of me? My God, would she suffer if she knew the cold I have to suffer, the dangers I have to face every moment of every day, what a calamity without hope of consolation this life on the run is, sleeping out in all kinds of weather, eating whatever comes to hand, hiding in any hole or cave full of hostile beasts? Would she know what it really is to live all alone, without making common cause with anyone, without being able to tell anyone about my love and my horror? . . .

And she? How would she be living? Who keeps her? How does she keep from dying of hunger? Who flirts with her now behind the window? What does she think about during the night when the others, together, leave her alone? Could she think about me? Would she think I'm thinking about her? Would she think that I'll soon be captured? She might think: *How long can he survive? Where will he sleep tomorrow night? How will he protect himself from the rain and the night watchman? How will he cover himself when his torn clothes fall off his body? How long can he survive?* . . . My God, would she think that I'm thinking about her? Can she be thinking about me, and can our thoughts in some way be blending together? In that case, are our thoughts more united than ever? Can we be more united than ever? Can she at least have understood how much I love her? Is there any space in her grief for my grief? Can she have understood me? Can she

120

have forgiven me? Can she know, as I do now, just what a great love really is? Can she know that despite everything I am almost happy because of having existed like this, hungry, a fugitive, condemned, and cornered, but knowing that somewhere she also exists and that for one reason or another she must think about me from time to time? . . . Yes, if not through herself then at least through me, Cecilia must know what a great love really is; and for that reason, in some way we are accomplices and even friends. And that is enough. Because a great love, in order to be one, not only cannot take place but cannot even be marred by that hope. Because a great love is neither rest nor satisfaction but renunciation, distance, and above all the torture that comes from realizing that the loved object must be happy even if we have to push the beloved into the arms of our rival. . . . Now that I have killed my rival, I understand it all.

New York
July 25, 1984